THE RELUCTANT ALPHA

WEST COAST WOLVES, BOOK ONE

SUSI HAWKE

Copyright © 2020 by Susi Hawke

All rights reserved.

Editing, proofreading, and formatting provided by LesCourt Author Services

Cover design by Cate Ashwood Designs

No part of this book may be reproduced in any form or by any electronic or mechanical means, including information storage and retrieval systems, without written permission from the author, except for the use of brief quotations in a book review.

THE RELUCTANT ALPHA

WEST COAST WOLVES, BOOK ONE

"As much as I felt bad for this Elisha person—God, my heart was breaking for the man and all he'd been through—I was also angry. I'd left that pack in my rearview ten years ago for a good reason."

Mattias Longclaw is happy living his life on the back of his beloved Harley with his five best friends and brothers-in-arms at his side. The West Coast Wolves are a rare pack of alphas, made up of unwanted orphans and second-born sons. The packs they were born to may not have wanted them, but they've built a solid family of their own. They help where they can, doing random acts of kindness and expecting nothing in return, just helping to build a world they want to live in.

Then Matt gets a call from an old childhood buddy. He's being called back—begged to return—to reclaim his birthright and save a life in the process. The problem is... to do it, he will have to take a mate. And if he refuses? The omega will die.

Torn between his duty to help others and his resentment of his old pack, Matt never expects for Elisha Whitetail to tilt his world and change everything. Can Matt and Elisha rebuild a broken pack while tending to a new love and a growing family while dealing with outside threats from neighboring packs?

They're wolves. Strong, proud, and willing to do what it takes when their community needs them... whatever it takes.

This is the first in a new series about finding joy in a hard world, building family, and discovering that life can surprise a person when they least expect it. Although this world has harsher themes than my previous books, it still has the same heart you'd expect. Plus a dose of my irreverent humor and all the naughty, knotty heat that comes with true mates. It wouldn't be a Susi Hawke book without it.

AUTHOR'S NOTE

This is the first in a new series of full-length books featuring a ragtag MC of alpha wolf shifters whose only pack is the one they've forged. The pack system in this world is more structured than in my previous books. There's only room for one alpha—and his heir—in each pack. Any other alpha sons are kicked out of the pack at age eighteen with a small payoff and a buh-bye from his sire. If an alpha heir doesn't accept his birthright, he is also free to leave when he reaches maturity. The "West Coast Wolves" are a group of castoff alpha sons who have found their own place with each other as they travel the west on their bikes, looking for adventure.

If you've read my books, you'll know I like my omegas to be sassy, brassy, and easily heard. In this world, however, omegas are second-class citizens, first owned by their sire and then by the alpha he sells or trades them to… but if they trust their alpha, or he's their true mate, they might just have a special secret or two that makes them invaluable. I hope you enjoy this new series. It's different from my other shifters, but you'll find the same heart I put into all my books.

I'd like to give a special thank you to Gabryyl Pierce from my Facebook group, The Hawke's Nest, for naming the special fangs only alphas possess. Hidden behind their canines, the laniary teeth only come down for two things—claiming their mates or killing an enemy—and then only at the alpha's will. His wolf determines whether the teeth deliver aconite for the mating bite or Medeina venom to paralyze and kill. Special thanks go to Sniege Gruode and Fran Stanton for naming the poisons. Sniege shared that Medeina is a she-wolf goddess from Lithuanian folklore, a fact that made me fall in love with using it for the venom.

Possible trigger warning for a scene of dubious consent where the alpha must claim his mate to break a prior bond that is now killing him, and the omega is too delirious to properly give consent. I promise it's not jarring, and the omega will be happy his life was saved.

xox, Susi

ONE

ELISHA

Hot. So hot. In my fevered state, the room was blurry and spinning. My clawed fingertips scraped at the sweat-soaked sheet before breaking the fabric of the goose down mattress topper.

I spat out a mouthful of the erupting feathers, falling like snow. Sneezing, my eyes grew more watery. How many times had I told Horace I was allergic to it?

A memory best left forgotten flashed through my mind. *Oh, yeah. I only told him once.* After the beating I received for not appreciating the lifestyle my alpha provided me, I hadn't dared mention it again.

Naturally, once I had enough clarity to remember the hated allergen I slept over every night, barely separated by a few layers of fabric, my rash started to itch.

Itchy. Groaning, I started to scratch my ass where the worst of the small red bumps covering my body clustered, only to scream in agony when my claws scored deep lines across my ass.

Whimpering now, my eyes swelled as I buried my face in the bedding and tried to ignore the burn. The salty sweat seeping into the fresh cuts was almost painful enough for me to forget how badly I still itched.

I needed to get out of this bed before it killed me. Ha. Like I wasn't about to die anyway. Jared had tried to downplay my fate, but it wasn't necessary. I knew the score.

The moment Horace bit the nape of my neck with his laniary teeth and injected the aconite in his mating bite, my life was linked to his. I wanted to live. Even more, I wanted my pup to live. But Horace was no longer breathing, and I couldn't quite summon any sadness.

My baby bump rubbed against the mattress when I tried to crawl away from the feathers. As bad as I hurt—actually ached with the pain searing from the very marrow of my bones—I would spend every moment I had left fighting to survive.

Jared had promised to try. He said he had a Hail Mary move, one I'd never expect and would not simply save my life but make it better. Whimpering, I was curled in a ball now, my body shaking with an unearthly chill signaling the beginning of my demise. The beta probably had no idea whether or not I'd heard him.

But I had. Every word of hope was burned into my brain. During these dwindling moments of clarity, I summoned them to remind myself to fight. Even now, Jared's soft voice repeated over the pulsing heartbeat pounding in my ears.

"My friend Matthias can save you. He should've been the alpha after his father died anyway. I have his number, and I will do all I can to beg him to step in." I hadn't understood why another alpha would possibly matter until he'd spoken a final thought before leaving me to my misery. "Isaac assured me—another alpha's bite is all it takes to end aconite poisoning."

I would live happily the rest of my life without ever being claimed by another alpha—if remaining alive was possible at all. Since fate had never been so kind to omegas, I'd long ago resigned myself to the necessity.

Maybe this next one, this Matthias, would be kinder. Maybe he wouldn't hit as hard. I didn't mind a few injuries. Broken bones mended after a shift, and a good herbal remedy would fix anything lingering. But not always being in pain would be nice. Not always being on the mend from yet another injury. Especially if he let me keep my pup. I would need my full strength to care for the baby.

Stretching, I managed to grab the iron rungs on the headboard. Gritting my teeth, I tried to pull myself away from the worst of the feathers. I didn't have enough strength to get off the bed, but if I could just heave myself toward the side, maybe I could roll off onto the floor.

A fresh searing pain took my breath away when my shoulder dislocated as I pulled. Either my muscles were too weak, or my body really was made of lead now. That's what it felt like.

No. Not lead. *Lava.*

Yes. Heavy, molten heat flooding through my body and turning it to stone.

Panting, I cleared another inch as I pushed toward my goal. How I would manage to sit up, I couldn't say yet. If I could keep myself awake long enough to get away from the feathers, I might find a little relief.

Relief from what? The room began to spin, and I forgot what I was worried about as the pain surged, and I felt myself drifting away.

Focus. You need to focus.

My wolf was alert, nagging me to pay attention to...

something. Was it the boys? Did my little brothers need help?

"Noah? Saul? Where are you? I can't help you if you hide..." I barely recognized the raspy sound of my own voice. Something was wrong.

Agh! A shock of pain made my muscles spasm, and I somehow ended up on my knees with my face smashed into the pillows. Flinging myself to the right, I flopped back onto my side and curled into a ball, resting my hands over my small baby bump as I tried to ignore the loud, keening cry surrounding me.

As my vision began to fade, my wolf nudged me awake enough to realize two things. Death wasn't far away... and the awful wailing was coming from me.

TWO

MATT

After a hard day's ride down the California coast, parking my bike and standing on solid ground again felt good. I had no guarantees of it staying this way. A scruffy honkytonk on the outskirts of Los Angeles was iffy on its best day. Not to mention the very real possibility of an earthquake.

Right now, I wasn't worried about either of those things. My wolf would sense if a quake was on the way, and the human bikers hanging around this joint wouldn't mess with us. While they'd never let us see them sweat, not even the toughest man in this place wanted to come up against me and my boys.

When five alpha wolves pulled up with matching cuts—complete with our own 'WCW' emblem proudly emblazoned across the back, letters arched over a snarling wolf—people tended to stay out of our way. Not because we were assholes or anything. Or because they had a clue shifters even existed. No, it was all in the vibe. While we might not have looked anything other than human, something about us made people nervous on a visceral level.

The little voice in the back of a person's head alerting them of danger or the gut feeling saying not to walk down a certain dark alley made sure the baddest sumbitches knew not to screw with us. Despite what people might have thought given our height and large muscles, none of us were bad guys. We were honestly pretty easygoing as a rule, unless we saw someone in need of protection.

Lacking a full home pack to defend didn't mean shit. Our wolves were wired to be protectors. Unfortunately, not all alphas were as sweet as we were. Wolf shifters were just like anyone, with free choice and individual personalities, and some alphas were real dicks. God only knew I'd met more than a few of them in the decade since I'd struck out on my own.

Plain luck brought the West Coast Wolves together. To a man, all five of us were ruled by a code of honor, making us look out for the weak and kick any and all bullies in the teeth. We rode together, we fought together, we bled together. We were the West Coast Wolves.

None of us was the leader. We worked together democratically, and we all liked it that way. I'd met the guys during my travels, after I'd abandoned my birthright as alpha heir to my home pack. My father was one of those dick alphas, and I hadn't liked the way he ran the pack with an iron fist. Or his home with a bloodier one.

Until I turned eighteen, my only claiming mark had been the scarred X over my heart where my father marked me at birth. As with all pups, it made me pack until I became an adult. At maturity, I got to choose. I could bend the knee and accept his claiming bite on the soft skin of my inner left wrist. To join the pack and prepare for the day I would become alpha. Otherwise, I could leave and never return. Hmm... his mark or my freedom. Turned out it wasn't as tough a choice as one might think. The beat-down my father gave me the night before my birthday, with the warning I'd 'better not fuck this up,' had been all the reminder I needed. I'd be better on my own.

Luckily, my maternal grandparents invited me over for a birthday breakfast. When they asked me whether I was going to bend the knee, I quietly told them no. My bruises and the swelling had already healed during the night after a quick shift to speed things along. But my grandparents didn't need proof to know my father liked to knock me around.

Still, I'd expected them to try and talk me out of it. Instead, my grandfather slipped me the key to a safe deposit box from a bank in Bakersfield and quietly explained my mother had a life insurance policy the alpha hadn't known about. She took it out herself and named her parents as the beneficiaries after she'd learned she was pregnant with me. Should anything happen to her, she'd instructed the money was to be kept for me.

While she couldn't have known she'd die before my first birthday, I could safely assume she wanted to make sure I'd be protected. As much as I would have liked to hope my father had treasured his mate and only became violent after losing her, my gut said otherwise. I tried not to think about it too much, but the worry was always in the back of my mind. Worry a woman—one who'd given me life, yet I had no memory of—had once been on the other end of the fists I knew all too well.

Shaking off my thoughts, I turned to see what my friends were doing. No. Not friends, *pack*. Devon, Tucker, and Nick were all secondary alpha sons who hadn't been given an option on their eighteenth birthdays of joining their home packs. Traditional thinking said having more than one alpha in a pack was dangerous, unless one was the heir. In accordance with the Supreme Council rules governing all American packs, they were turned loose at eighteen with ten percent of their father's worth as payoff to leave and never return.

As much as their lives sucked, they had it better than Lucian. His sire refused to claim him at birth—marking him forever as a bastard because he lacked the faded X scar over his heart. Lucian grew up in foster care after being turned over to the Territory Chief of our state. Until he came of age, he was moved from pack to pack, never allowed to spend more than six months with anyone. Since California had seventy-three officially recognized packs to choose from, Lucian had seen his share of the Golden State.

He wasn't affected, at least not so anyone could see. Lucian was always prepared with a joke and a smile. The flirtatious shit was already standing in the doorway with a hot twink on one arm and a sexy mama in the other. As he walked by, Nick elbowed me in the ribs. "Is it too early to lay odds on which one he ends up with tonight?"

Snorting, Tucker came up beside me. "Come on, Nick. It's Lucian we're talking about, remember? Even money says he tries for both." Nick and I both grinned because he had a good point. As wolves, we were inherently bisexual. And as alpha wolves? We were plain highly sexual in general. As far as I could tell, Lucian had a double dose in the libido department. Part of me had always wondered if Lucian was really so horny or if he was hoping his true mate would accidentally fall on his cock one of these days.

A guy who'd been alone since birth probably didn't want to stay solo forever. Either way, the dude's bedroom had a revolving door. Or it would if he had one, which he didn't, since we lived our lives on the road. I didn't judge, though. He was my friend, my pack mate. Whatever made him happy was good with me.

We were definitely a pack. Maybe not one the Supreme Council recognized, but a pack nonetheless. While we rode up and down the highways, we had each other's backs through good times and bad. We cheered each other on, and any one of us would take a bullet for another. If we weren't pack by anyone's standards, then maybe my dictionary had a different definition.

Nick followed Lucian inside, his arm automatically going around another sexy mama watching him approach. Tucker said hello to a grizzled old-timer who was straddling his bike and picking what looked like a few days' worth of dead bugs out of his long yellowish-white beard. *Lovely.* I never let my beard grow longer than my helmet, if I had one. Personally, I avoided facial hair because I didn't like the way my helmet rubbed against the scruff.

Blowing a slow whistle as he checked out the old-timer's bike, Devon ambled over to join us. "Nice ape hangers, man. Couldn't handle it myself. Vibration has got to be hard on the shoulders."

The guy didn't seem as spooked by us as other bikers normally were. Probably because he was old enough to be ornery if he wanted and didn't give a shit who cared. Grunting, he stopped picking his beard to smirk at Devon. "It takes a real man to handle a beauty like this, son. If you can't handle the vibes, maybe you don't belong on the road."

Devon—ever the peacekeeper—kept a congenial smile on his face. "Maybe so, but I think I do all right. Haven't wiped out or gotten any cases of road rash in recent memory, so I guess I'll keep riding. I like your bedroll. Bet it makes a great bug shield. Made it yourself, did ya?"

He knew the magic words to get the old-timer talking.

The two of them discussed the man's bedroll while Tucker and I wandered inside.

We grabbed the last empty pool table, and I racked the balls while he went to get a couple beers. At the bar, Lucian was parked at one end with the twink on one leg and the sexy mama on the other. The two didn't seem too interested in each other but sure were focused on Lucian... and competing for his attention. From the looks of it, he had his hands full. Nick was on the dance floor trolling for a date for the night. Whenever Devon made it inside, he'd probably end up shooting the breeze with whoever was sitting next to him once he claimed a barstool. And Tucker and I would play pool.

I knew how things would go down because they always went the same way. The only changes we typically saw in our day-to-day lives were the scenery we rolled past and which bar we ended up in. Otherwise, we were creatures of habit.

Halfway through our third game, Tucker poked my buzzing ass with his pool stick. "Okay, whoever keeps calling isn't going to stop. You might be able to ignore it—hell, maybe you're enjoying the vibrating action—but dammit, answer your fucking phone before I snatch it out of your pocket and snap it in half."

I rolled my eyes and pulled my phone out. "Right. Because you'd really be so drastic. Nah, I figure anyone I need to talk to is inside these four walls. It's probably a wrong number anyway."

Grinning, Tucker motioned for me to hurry up and deal with the call. "So answer it and tell the poor schmuck whatever chick he bought a drink for last week obviously gave him a wrong number. And hurry up because I'm about to kick your ass again when I bank the eight ball off the side and hit the corner pocket."

"Doubt it." I frowned at my screen, relieved the call had gone to voicemail but chilled when I saw the Lucerne Valley area code. The good old 760... my hometown.

Tucker must've noticed something in my expression because he immediately stiffened as if on the alert. "Trouble?"

"Not sure. Area code is for my home pack or someone in the general area. Don't know how they'd have my number when my grandparents passed several years ago. Can't think of anyone there I'd like to talk to either, to be honest." With my bad blood in mind, I deleted all the voice messages without listening to them. Screw that shit. I didn't need to hear from my father if he'd somehow gotten a hold of my number, and I couldn't think of anyone else who would try to reach me because I'd been gone for over a decade.

When my phone vibrated with the same number, Tucker scratched his jaw. "Want me to answer? I have no problem telling your old man to fuck right off. He's neither my sire nor my alpha, so it's no skin off my nose. But whether you do it or I do, someone has to answer, or he's gonna keep calling. If it's even your father. You never know—maybe he got challenged, and there's a new alpha in town. Or one of your childhood friends has been pining for your sweet ass all these years and wants to beg you to come get them."

"I seriously doubt anyone's calling to pledge their undying love. And if it's a new alpha, then he can sit and spin too. I'm telling you, there's no good reason for anyone to be calling from Lucerne Valley. Especially out of the fucking blue. Nothing they can say would possibly have any impact on my life."

"Then answer the damn phone. Or let me do it. Come on, Matt. At this point, the curiosity alone is killing me." Yeah... *no*. I was not going to have another alpha deal with my shit. I could handle it, whatever it was. Maybe.

"Fine. Only so you'll quit whining like a little girl." I accepted the call, immediately putting it to my ear as I answered with a growl. "If you're looking for Matthias, you've got him."

A voice I hadn't heard since right after it deepened surprised me. "Matty? Sorry. I meant to say Matthias. Thank the goddess you finally answered! This is Jared. I'm not sure if you remember me, but I'm pack beta now and the captain of the pack council."

"Shit, like I could ever forget you. How the hell are you doing, Jared? And more importantly, how did you get my number? I don't want to make things awkward, but I don't want my father to have it."

Jared sucked in a breath. "I know your grandparents left the pack when you did, but they stayed in touch with my parents. Didn't they tell you? Matty... your Uncle Horace challenged your father about six months after you left. As for your number, your grandmother gave it to me in case there was ever an emergency."

Stunned, I leaned back against the pool table and rubbed a hand over my mouth. All these years, and my father had been dead nearly the whole time. I understood why they hadn't told me. A brother challenging his own family member and giving the killing bite was horrifying. My father was a dick, but even he didn't deserve such a death. Thanks to the tradition forcing him to strike out on his own at eighteen, I'd never met my uncle.

Hmm... maybe there was a reason for only keeping one alpha son around. Biology could be a bitch. Either that or the packs could, I don't know, teach their alpha sons to coexist.

But then again, my father never had a good word to say about his brother Horace. According to him, Horace was a sniveling coward who couldn't be trusted. The type of alpha who fought dirty and stabbed people in the back. I'd always figured my dad was simply being his not-so-charming self, but now it sounded like he'd been telling the truth.

Jared was quiet for several moments as if realizing I'd needed to absorb the idea. I took a deep breath and forced myself back to the conversation. "I appreciate you calling, Jared. But if you want me to come challenge my uncle, then it's not gonna happen. This apple fell and rolled far away from the poisonous tree. I'm sorry, but Lucerne Valley doesn't have a hold on me anymore. My uncle can have fun being alpha. I made my peace years ago."

"Your uncle's not why I am calling, Matthias." When he spoke in a more serious tone and used my formal name again, a spike of dread punched me in the gut. "He's dead. Do you remember Monty Whitetail, the alpha of the Newberry Springs pack? He challenged Alpha Horace in retaliation—or so he said—for stealing Monty's omega son and mating him against his will. As of yesterday, your uncle is gone, and the pack and all its holdings officially belong to the Newberry Springs pack."

At the thought of anyone related to me doing such a thing, my blood ran cold. "You don't need to play word games with me, Jared. I'm a straight shooter, so tell me the truth. Did my uncle really do it? Did Monty have the right to challenge him?"

Jared hesitated, then sighed ever so softly in my ear. "Sorry, I'm so used to having to watch everything I say. Yes. As much as it pains me to admit it. I don't have proof your uncle stole him, but I heard the poor omega's anguished screams the night Alpha Horace brought him home. And my quarters are downstairs and in the east wing. Matty... shoot. I hate to put this on you, but Alpha Mate Elisha needs you."

I froze, unable to make a sound because I knew full well what was coming next. I felt a hand on my shoulder and swallowed at the concern on Tucker's face. Jerking my chin to let him know I was okay, I forced myself to talk.

"Trust me, Jared. I'm not at all what Elisha needs. If his father won the challenge, then he can go home, and his father can find him a mate of his choosing. I'm sorry our pack will be disbanded and absorbed into Newberry Springs, but the law's pretty clear if the challenge was legal and witnessed by the Territory Chief Alpha. You know the rules as well as I do."

"Matthias, it's not so easily solved, or I wouldn't be calling. Elisha was pregnant when your uncle died. You know what a severed bond means for an omega. A bonded omega will follow his alpha into the grave within three days if left unclaimed. Usually, the challenger gives him a new bite if victorious, but it was his own father, so... *yeah*. Not an option in this case. Without a new bond, both he and the child he carries will be dead within three days. This is day two, and he's already gone into a delirium. I doubt he'll last another day without a fresh mating bite. It's the curse of biology, and we all know it."

As much as I felt bad for this Elisha person—goddess, my heart broke for the man and all he'd been through—I was also angry. I'd left my pack in my rearview ten years ago for a good reason. They all witnessed my father's brutal treatment of me and looked the other way.

Understandably so, since he was the alpha. But a kind

word or gentle smile here and there would've gone a long way. Instead, they ignored me, even when my father wasn't around. Jared had been my single friend growing up, solely because his father had been the pack beta before him.

Shit. In order for Jared to be beta, his father would've had to die. My anger deflated. Titus and Paula, Jared's parents, had always treated me well. If not for them, I wasn't sure I would've survived my childhood—at least not with my soul intact. I sucked in a breath and blew it out slowly. Though I'd let go of the anger, I wasn't ready to give in easily, so I may have sounded harsh when I spoke again.

"Why should I care, Jared? Why am I the one who needs to come save this man? I don't want Elisha to die, but I'm also not in the market for a mate or a pack. And let's not forget you're not merely asking me to claim him. If I do this, I will have to challenge and kill his father to get our pack back. Unless Monty will gift it to his son, which I don't really see happening. No offense, but this isn't a small favor you're asking from me."

Jared wasn't offended, or maybe he was more focused on the outcome than on what was said getting there. "Matty, Elisha didn't ask to be your uncle's mate. When he was taken and forcibly claimed, he was barely of age. Think about it like this—your uncle was worse than our old alpha, so what kind of a life do you think he's had here? And now he's pregnant and was left to die by his own father? While I know most alphas wouldn't care about some omega and his pup, I believe you would. Do you, old friend? Or have you changed so radically in the years since you've gone?"

Dammit. The guy was good at negotiating—and emotional blackmail—I'd give him some credit. Not only had he called me Matty, but he *had* to tack on 'old friend.' Tucker, standing close enough to easily hear both halves of the conversation, shook his head. I didn't know whether he was telling me to stand my ground or reminding me of our code.

Fuck me, I don't have a choice. I have to do this, no matter how much it kills me. Nevertheless, I tried one more time to beg off.

"You ask too much, Jared. This is unfair. You want me to come back and fight to retake the pack from Monty—since we both know he won't hand it over—*and* you are asking me to forcibly claim a delirious omega who was already abused by my uncle. And then you want me to accept the responsibility of his pup, too. Is that what you're saying? Feel free to correct me if I'm wrong."

Jared spoke in a rush, relief evident in his voice when he realized there was a chance I would give in. "There's just no other way, Matty. Newberry Springs invaded this morning. Half of our Delta soldiers were killed, and the others were either taken or left to die. Isaac—our current epsilon healer—saved the ones he could. I have all the wounded here, along with the four gammas from our ruling council."

He paused barely long enough to take a breath. "We've sequestered ourselves in the alpha mansion. Monty and his men left a few hours ago with every able man and boy of working age. They took them back to Newberry Springs, leaving women and children and the elderly or physically challenged men behind. About thirty-one pack members remain, aside from the council and the injured deltas. Matty, I'm turning to you because I don't know what else to do. I can't protect them and the alpha mate at the same time. And I certainly can't claim him. I need help from a real alpha who I can trust to save both Elisha and our pack."

When I heard Monty had left his son behind, I knew

immediately I would do as Jared asked. I still had a few questions, though.

"Jared, I remember Monty Whitetail as being a hardass. But surely he didn't mean to basically murder his own son? Especially when he's pregnant? He knows about the pup, doesn't he? Exactly how long has my uncle had this omega there? I've calmed down, so I'm thinking our packs are no more than an hour apart. Why didn't Monty save his son sooner? I mean, he has to have been there at least a few weeks, right? Detecting the pregnancy before then would've been impossible unless your healer stumbled over it during an examination or something."

As if it broke his heart to say the words, Jared spoke solemnly. "Your uncle brought Elisha here over six months ago. His father had more than enough time to find and rescue him. The truth is, he's been negotiating with Alpha Horace for a payout. When our Alpha didn't meet his terms, Monty threw down the challenge. Understand this, Matthias. Monty doesn't want Elisha back. He told me—and this is a direct quote—to *let the mutt die*. He said his only worth was as a bartering chip for a pact he'd been trying to make with an alpha in Arizona. Their deal fell through when Elisha was stolen, and Monty focused on getting some sort of payback from Alpha Horace. Now Monty has everything he wants and no reason to rescue someone he considers used goods."

"Fuck! I have to do this, don't I?" I was speaking more to myself than to Jared.

"We need you, Matty. We need you to save Elisha and to save our pack. We could've used your leadership for years. But now you're our last hope. I know I'm asking a lot, but the pack we have now aren't the same people who were here when you left. Most of our parents' generation either moved along after Alpha Horace came into power or have died out. The ones here now are mostly a mix of new blood and the people we grew up with.

You might not have to kill Monty, you know. You could offer a ceremonial challenge, where whoever strikes first blood wins, and wrest control of the pack without any blood on your hands. But if you did have to kill him, Elisha wouldn't blame you. And you'll like Elisha, I mean it. He's young, but he's an old soul with a gentle sweetness about him. Oh, and he's a great cook. A real homebody... but then, I've heard most omegas are pretty shy."

"You don't have to sell me on his qualities as a mate, Jared. Even if he was a complete asshole, I would still be willing to save his life. He's the victim here, and I damned well know it." Sighing, I pushed away from the pool table and paced back and forth. I didn't want to do this but... *shit*. There was no other choice.

Considering everything Jared said, I felt better about the decision I was about to make, though I had to ramble through my thoughts. "I'd be within my rights whether I chose the ceremonial or traditional challenge. Either way, I would avenge my uncle's death, as heinous as the idea sounds. And I would be asserting my rights on behalf of my new mate and his unborn child. If I'm the one who acts, the Supreme Council won't have a reason to intervene. The Territory Chief will sign off on it without question. Dammit. I really *was* your only option."

Jared spoke softly, his voice thick with emotion. "There is nobody else, old friend. But even if there were, you're the most trustworthy alpha I've ever met. Being your pack beta would be my honor." With a soft sigh, he paused for a second. "Matty, I hate to ask this of you, but we need you—Elisha *needs* you—and time grows short."

"Give me an hour and a half to get there. And Jared? Thank you for giving a shit. But do me a favor? I don't like the idea of the weaker pack members being left unguarded in town while you and the gammas are sequestered. Tell those gamma wolves to get off their asses and go get every leftover pack member. I want them behind the safety of those walls, and I want it done before I get there, or my first act as alpha will be finding some new gammas."

Jared chuckled lightly. "There's the alpha I remember. Hurry home, Matty. It's been far too long."

THREE

MATT

As I rolled through my hometown, whatever tension I felt about returning to Lucerne Valley quickly turned into anger. I wasn't sure what I expected, but it wasn't finding the place in shambles. Even under the darkness of night, thanks to a full moon and sharp wolf vision, everything was as clear as if the sun was up.

When I left, our pack had enjoyed a well-maintained, bustling community. We were located about thirty miles, as the crow flies, from the place shown on California maps as Lucerne Valley. But to find our much smaller town—it didn't really have a name other than Longclaw Packlands—you had to know which dirt road to take through the expanse of desert we called home.

In order to truly comprehend what I was seeing, I had to slow down and stop. Shops with boarded-over windows and tattered canopies flapping in the wind. Overgrown plots of land where community gardens and play areas used to be. Heart sinking, I kickstarted my bike and began moving again.

The small clusters of homes showed no pride in ownership. Peeling paint, sagging roofs and dirty windows, filthy from the last sandstorm, made the place look like the world's poorest ghost town. None of the scraggly yards I passed featured so much as a bike thrown down in a front yard or a random ball.

The more I saw, the sicker I felt. Would bringing this community back to life be possible if I did manage to retake it from Monty? Shaking my head, I sped up and rode uphill when I reached the edge of town. As soon as I caught a glimpse of the gated alpha mansion, I was ready to punch something.

How could any pack Alpha have thought living in splendor was okay while his people didn't seem to have the most basic of their needs met? Here, where every window glowed with well-lit rooms, I realized what else had been missing back in town. If Jared had brought the pack here like I'd asked, it made sense if none of the houses had lights on. But the shops? No, not even one of the stores had so much as a blinking sign either.

Was the pack so poor or frugal the stores no longer bothered with security lights, or was what I suspected the real truth? Surely, the alpha mansion wasn't the only place with electricity around here.

Growling under my breath, I stopped in front of the gate and tried my old gate code on the keypad. Surprisingly, it actually worked, and the gate slid open. With an angry kick, I got my bike moving again and revved my engine, taking off like a shot up the driveway.

I parked and turned off the engine, removing my helmet and cursing my uncle's name as I got a better look at the perfectly maintained property. Here, there was a nice green lawn, and the paint job was as fresh as the day the old place was built. I was still grumbling under my breath and wishing it were possible to bring Alpha Horace back to life so I could choke it out of him again when the front door swung open.

An older but nonetheless completely familiar-looking face smiled back at me, and I found myself grinning and waving like a damn fool. "Jared! Goddess, but it is good to see you." I got off the bike and stashed my gloves and helmet before running up the stairs to greet him with a hug. We clasped each other tight, and for a brief moment, being home felt good again.

Jared didn't allow me more than a minute. Before I finished processing how much taller and thicker he was in the shoulders, he was already pulling away and motioning for me to follow. One look at his pinched expression reminded me of the reason I broke every speed limit to get here. The pack and what it needed would have to wait. Right now, Elisha's life depended on me.

When Jared covered his mouth with a rough sob, my heart fell into my stomach. I staggered back a step, holding my palms up in denial. "No. Tell me I'm not too late?" Before I could ask another question, a strangled cry from overhead gave me my answer—the omega lived.

Taking a breath, I willed my anxious wolf into submission. The sucker paced and clawed at my skin, demanding to take over, the one thing I couldn't allow. With this much at stake, my human side needed to be in control.

Sorry, wolfie. Stand down. I've got this one.

Jared winced and tilted his head toward the stairs. "Again, I'm sorry to put you in this position. And for my display of emotion. It's just that... Isaac, our epsilon healer... I believe I mentioned him when we last spoke? He had a vision during the winter solstice, saying our pack would find salvation and renewal this year. His words came back to me while I was waiting for you to get here. Seeing you now, I know his vision signaled your return. I just hate the burden I've placed on your shoulders with what I'm asking of you."

Knowing even as I spoke how I meant every word, I straightened my shoulders and stood tall. "You didn't put this on me, Jared. This pack was always my birthright, and it's past time I accepted it. Do I want to claim Elisha in this state? No. Hell no. But he didn't ask for this any more than I did. I won't allow him to die because my uncle was a piece of shit." I started to say more, wanting to linger rather than face the task ahead of me.

Another loud, mournful cry had my wolf pacing again. Glancing at Jared with a clipped nod, I muttered, "Wish me luck," and strode away before he could respond. Heading straight to the stairs, I took them two at a time, sudden haste pushing me every step of the way.

My wolf and I both felt the same pull, demanding we get to the master bedroom as quickly as possible. I didn't understand it, but it was as if my own life depended on saving this omega's.

Move. Get there faster.

Every second felt like an eternity. Each cry sounding through the bedroom door felt like a steel blade piercing my heart. And yet I stopped short of opening it when I got there, pausing with one hand on the doorknob and one palm on the solid wood separating me from whatever I would find on the other side.

As badly as I needed to reach Elisha, I also needed this final moment to prepare myself. Consent from an omega in heat was dubious at best. But from one who was delirious and at death's door? Any yes he gave would be meaningless. Did I have it in me to do it anyway? Could I really fuck this stranger to save his life? And even worse... could I stomach giving him the claiming bite and forging his life to my own?

It was too much responsibility. And if I were to die tomorrow, he would be right back in this position.

Shut up, idiot. Quit trying to talk yourself out of what you know you're already planning to do. You wouldn't be here if you weren't going to claim this omega as your mate. Quit waffling and alpha up. Elisha's life is depending on you.

Whether it was my persuasive self-talk or the bloodcurdling scream I heard next, I couldn't say. But the terrifying shriek had me shoving the door open. One step into the room and I nearly hit my knees, staggering at a wave of omega pheromones and an enticing fragrance smelling of home... and a curious mix of jasmine and sagebrush.

Was it possible?

No... and yet there it was.

The powerful aroma could only be one thing—the scent of my true mate.

All my life I had searched for the place I truly belonged. This pack hadn't ever felt like my home, and neither had any place I'd spent more than a night in since I'd left here. Nothing had ever been a perfect fit. I'd come close enough with my fellow West Coast Wolves, but something had always been missing.

Not something... *someone*. Home wasn't a place. Home was here, with this stranger whose life depended on me getting my shit together and saving him while I could.

Move, dammit.

As I slowly inched closer, I had the presence of mind to kick the door shut, cataloging the destroyed bed. Gouges marked the mattress as if it had been clawed. Tiny feathers were all over, as if the ceiling had opened and snowed teeny tiny bits of fluff.

The fucking shit covered everything, including the whimpering omega curled in a tiny ball. I couldn't see his face behind his curtain of hair. With the snowfall of down, it was hard to see much of him at all.

A few feathers floated freely, drifting up and hovering before falling, only to shoot back up every time Elisha trembled. Others clung to his body like dried-up spitballs, stuck to his sweaty skin. The sheets were a twisted mess, as if Elisha had been kicking and shoving them away. Or tried to make an escape rope? Yeah, no.

My eyes went back to the feathers.

Something about them bothered my wolf. What were those things? Goose down or some shit. Who cared? Not me. All I knew was they needed to be gone. Something about them was... *bad.* Wolfie snarled, demanding we get our mate away from them. But first, I wanted... no, *needed*, to get a better look at my soon-to-be mate.

I drew closer to the bed, intending to pull the sweaty hair back covering his cheeks and forehead, but my hand stopped midair when I got a better look at his body. An acrid stench of sickness mixed with the coppery smell of dried blood had been hiding beneath his sweet scents of jasmine and sagebrush.

His body was covered with a rash. It didn't seem contagious or anything, but the clusters of red bumps didn't look comfortable. Blowing a strong breath out, I sent enough feathers flying to reveal more of his body and exactly how angry his skin looked.

Scratch marks on the curve of his ass provided the source for the blood. I sucked in a breath, unable to imagine itching awful enough to make a man scratch with clawed hands.

Or had he known? *Hmm...* it was hard to say. His wolf

must have been near the surface, no doubt doing his part in the fight to keep him alive. Another keening cry sounded, this one softer yet so laced with pain it hit me harder than the one I'd heard outside the door.

My stomach clenched. I knew what I needed to do, but I really didn't want to claim my fated mate like this. And yet, fuck watching him die. If I hadn't been willing to let a perfect stranger pass away, then I damn sure wouldn't, knowing who he was to me.

But still. Would reaching him in this condition be possible? I had to try. Even though every second of delay pushed him closer to the grave, I needed to know I'd at least tried to make him aware. Given him a chance to consent.

Carefully, I sat at the edge of the bed and leaned over him, finally pulling the hair back from his face. My breath caught at his beauty. Omegas were so rare I'd seen no more than one or two in my entire life. They were known to be pretty and delicate creatures, but Elisha was almost too lovely for description. His dark eyebrows were the same chestnut as his long, thick hair. His features were finely sculpted with high cheekbones and a narrow nose, and his rough, cracked lips were bow-shaped and full. Or would have been, if he were properly hydrated.

My wolf took only a second to imprint on our mate and memorize his features. Ignoring my wolf's howl echoing through my head, I studied the thick lashes curling up from Elisha's closed eyelids. At this moment, I couldn't think of anything I wanted more than seeing those eyes open. What color would they be? Would they sparkle with intelligence and humor or be dulled from all the pain and horror his body had experienced?

Stupid question, genius. Dull with pain at the moment.

So how about we get him out of said pain, so they have a chance to sparkle with humor at some future point?

Gently brushing the back of my knuckles along his exposed cheek, I fought to keep my voice level and hide the anguish that would tell him exactly how bad of shape he was in. I had no idea if he was alert enough to read subtleties of tone, if even on a subconscious level, but didn't want to risk it.

"Elisha? I'm your new alpha. My name is Matthias. Can you wake up, honey?"

When his sole answer was a whimper, I leaned closer. His chest and abdomen rolled with each short breath as if his body struggled to get enough air. I startled back when he snarled and claws erupted from his fingertips. He thrashed, moving to scratch a patch of red bumps on his stomach where a clump of feathers were stuck to his sweaty flesh.

"No. Stop, now." I couldn't help the dominant alpha warning and accompanying growl. Protecting my mate was of utmost importance. *If even from himself.* Elisha's hands paused, trembling as they poised just over his pregnant belly.

His eyes opened.

Not much. Definitely not enough to get a sense of eye color. The hair on the back of my neck lifted when I felt his wolf watching me, but Elisha himself was too out of it to know who I was or would be to him.

His eyes weren't opening all the way because they were puffy and half-swollen. Something about those eyes triggered a memory. Several years ago, there had been a boy. I frowned, knowing this information was important, but I had to strain to bring it to mind.

What was bugging me? The boy... why was I picturing his young face?

That's right!

Shit. I remembered it clearly now. A boy at a park up near Sacramento had been stung by a bee and had an allergic reaction. The EpiPen Lucian produced had helped save him, but such tactics wouldn't work here. Of this, I felt sure. Elisha needed to be removed from the allergen. Quick, fast, and in a hurry. Wincing, I noticed the feathers stuck to the bloody claw marks on his butt.

Fuck. If this guy didn't have bad luck, he wouldn't have any at all, it seemed. Having an allergen touch his skin was bad enough, but in direct contact with his blood? Definitely not okay. I whipped off my jacket and flung it to the side, pulling my phone from my pocket as I toed off my shoes.

Jared answered on the first ring. "M-Matty? Why are you calling me? Is everything okay up there?"

Growling, I kicked my shoe, sending it flying toward a dresser across the room. "No. Everything is not okay. I'm taking Elisha into the bathroom, and we will be in the shower. By the time I get out, I would like the mattress and all of these goddamned feathers removed from the room. In addition to the aconite poisoning from the mating curse, it seems he's also allergic to his own fucking bed. Can you fix it fast? Or maybe there's another room where I can take him?"

Yes. Another room sounded better. A fresh room for a fresh start.

"Not a problem. I can have it fixed within ten minutes. There's another bed the perfect size, in the guestroom we use when the territory chief or someone of his stature comes to visit. The mattress is brand new and won't take much to swap out."

I considered the concept, too frazzled to think clearly

about the layout of the mansion. "How far away is this guestroom? Is it in this wing?"

"Yes, it's on the opposite end of the hall. Remember? It's across from your childhood bedroom. If you want to move and are worried about either of you being seen, don't worry. You have privacy because you're alone on the floor right now. I'll wait until I hear from you to proceed, okay?"

Did I want to claim my mate in the room he had shared with my uncle, where he experienced so many traumatic events? There was no question.

"Thank you, Jared. I will be moving my mate to the guest suite, which you may consider to be the new Alpha chambers. Do not allow anyone in this area while my mate is naked and vulnerable. I would hate for them to meet my wolf in full protection mode." I started to end the call, then remembered my manners. "Oh, and thanks, Jared. I'll be in touch."

I shoved my phone back in my pocket and scooped Elisha up. Holding him against my chest, I carried him bridal-style. I felt better with every step taking us away from his awful bed and away from a room stinking of hovering death.

Although I knew where the guest suite was located, this might as well have been a different home than the one I'd lived in. Everything was updated and far fancier and lusher than my father ever would've had. Nothing in the hall was familiar. Even the paint color had changed since I lived here, but muscle memory took me straight to my old room and past it to the old guest suite.

How had I forgotten its existence? Easy. My father had never needed it, having had no use for making nice with the territory chief or the supreme council.

The guest room was cold and lifeless, if well decorated.

The single scent I picked up was a faint trace of lemon polish and a whiff of whoever had last cleaned in here. *Good.* A blank slate was exactly what Elisha and I needed.

I nudged the switch with my elbow, flooding the room with light before kicking the door shut. It was a large, well-appointed suite with a king-size bed to my left and a small sitting area straight ahead, arranged to enjoy the view from a multi-paned picture window. None of the details mattered at the moment. I only noticed a large dresser to my right when I nearly walked smack into it after I spotted the open bathroom door.

Yes. A shower. Perfect to get all these damn feathers off Elisha's body.

I couldn't care less about the deluxe bathroom or the floor which heated beneath my feet almost as soon as I hit all three switches next to the door, rather than figuring out which one operated the light.

The one thing I was pleased about was the huge walk-in shower, standing beside a bathtub wide enough for two. Elisha shivered, his body trembling harder from the cold air. Making soothing sounds, I reached into the shower and got the warm water flowing.

Reluctantly, I settled Elisha on a built-in bench inside the door. He curled right up, his knees flush against his baby bump as he huddled and rocked. I rested a hand on the top of his head. "*Shh*, easy now. You're safe, little wolf. Give me two seconds to get my britches off, and we'll get you cleaned up."

If I'd thought to grab my bag from the storage compartment on my bike and had a change of clothes, I wouldn't have even worried. I winced at the thunk when my jeans hit the floor and remembered my phone in the pocket. Oops. Good thing I hadn't walked into the shower fully clothed.

As soon as I had my shirt over my head, I let it drop behind me and went straight in. Scooping Elisha back up, I put him under the water and tried to get him to stand. "Come on, honey. Lower your legs and get on your feet so we can get you clean." I tried to get his body to respond, gently pushing at his knees as I murmured in his ear, "Please work with me, Elisha. We need to get this shit off your skin."

Nope. Nothing. He burrowed his face into my shoulder as he tried to curl into a tighter ball against my chest.

Even though I tried again, no amount of alpha persuasion in my tone worked. "Sorry, little wolf. I know you're in pain, but we really need to get these feathers off your body. I don't know if you can hear me, but your wolf can. I need you to stand. Do it for me now."

Still nothing. My own wolf paced desperately. We were on a tight clock to claim and save our mate, but I couldn't stomach doing it covered in an allergen causing him pain. No. I would save him, but I would make it as painless as possible. There was time. If there wasn't, surely the fates wouldn't be so cruel as to have brought me here.

Lowering myself to the floor, I decided to come at this from another direction. I cradled him in one arm, grabbing the detachable sprayer and rinsing the detestable feathers away. Thank heavens the drain had big openings, or we probably would have had a flood to deal with, based on how many clumps washed off.

Shifting his body this way and that, I managed to get every bit of his skin feather free. I was glad to see a bottle of the odorless body wash preferred by shifters, naturally hypoallergenic thanks to its pure, organic formula. While it might not have been his preference if he were awake, I also used it to shampoo his hair after his body was clean.

I sat him up between my legs and crossed my ankles over his, holding them in place while I gently massaged the lather into his hair. My wolf paced faster, anxious for me to move things along and claim our mate. Especially while his life force was hanging by a thread. A frayed thread I could feel unraveling.

My gut said I had time, though, and I needed to take it, to know the sick smell and any lingering allergens from his feather exposure were gone. Plus, I felt much better about what I had to do next after taking a few minutes to gently cleanse his body.

Elisha might not have been aware, but I was. Brute force was not my style. Neither was nonconsensual sex. This small bit of tender caretaking was necessary if I was going to have a chance of carrying through. Of doing this permanent deed under such unthinkable circumstances.

You're waffling again. Knock it off! It's time.

Elisha started shaking, so hard his ass vibrated against my cock. Shameful though it might have been, damned but if it didn't get me hard. Wondering if the body wash could double as lube, I wrapped an arm around his waist and bent him forward as I lifted him.

His cheeks parted barely enough to reveal a pink hole. Blinking in confusion, I realized it was glistening with something thick and viscous... and definitely not the body wash.

What the hell? Hadn't I cleaned him well?

As I slowly understood, a smile spread over my face. The slick I'd always heard an omega's body released if they were ready to be mounted was a relief to see. At least I could take comfort in knowing I wouldn't hurt him.

As I lowered him, I held him firmly by the hips with both hands while using my fingers to spread his cheeks.

My breath caught in my throat, and I grit my teeth

against the onslaught of pleasure when the head of my cock pierced through his tight ring of muscles, entering his slick heat at last.

Shaking harder, Elisha bucked back and forth, hands flapping at his sides. I jerked my head away to avoid getting hit when his head suddenly flung backward, aiming right at my face.

With my cock partially inside him, I quickly moved my hands as his body continued lowering onto mine. Wrapping an arm back around his waist, I held my other hand against his chest, settling him tightly against my shoulder so neither of us would get hurt.

While I fought to restrain my mate's shaking body, I somehow got him fully seated. Heart racing, I froze when Elisha's heavy panting stopped, along with the shaking, as his small frame slumped against mine.

Shit! Had I wasted too much time washing his hair? Fuck me, please tell me I hadn't waited too long to act. Immediately, when I started to really panic, my wolf nudged me, and I realized Elisha's heart was beating beneath my palm.

It was faint. Weak, even. But it was there.

The reassurance sent me into a frenzy, and I bucked my hips, thrusting fast and sure. I could make love to my mate another time. A time when he was alert and aware of what was happening. Right now, Elisha didn't need more from me than the quick, hard fuck to save his life.

Hugging him tightly, I fucked into him with such quick, firm movements the muscles in my own ass and legs would be feeling it tomorrow.

As his silky heat gripped my cock like a velvet glove, the walls clenching around my shaft so perfectly as if we'd been designed for each other, my inhibitions faded. My hips continued to rock, my muscles trembling from the exertion.

Ignoring the fire sliding through my veins and the lightning shooting down my spine, I kept going. My balls grew tight, pulling against my body, and the base of my cock tingled, stretching with my bulging knot.

The knot grew fat, completely locking me inside my mate. As my laniary teeth extended with my canines, I dropped my jaw. Both sets were needed, my wolf and I each providing part of the claiming bite.

Shifting Elisha to the left, I held his hair out of the way while I bit over the scar of his first mating, replacing his wrongful mark forever with my own. As my teeth pierced his flesh, Elisha gasped, his back stiffening and his head dropping forward as if welcoming my bite.

My balls clenched, and my seed shot inside his tight, welcoming heat. A sharp pain arced through my sinuses as the aconite flowed from the pinpoint-sized holes at the tips of my laniary fangs. While my body was motionless and stiff as Elisha's, my wolf delivered the poison, not merely saving his life but tethering it to mine.

Now, in this moment, I was finally okay with the idea. The bond settled between us, forming an unseverable connection. Even if I would never be able to understand why biology had provided us with this lover's poison, my possessive wolf was proud we had claimed Elisha.

But that wasn't why I was okay with it.

No. The softly whispered words, spoken in a raspy voice filled with wonder, settled my remaining concerns. "Mate. You... *came*. You saved me."

Carefully, I retracted my teeth, first licking the wound to hasten healing before pressing a gentle kiss to the bite mark. My biceps were relieved when I relaxed my tight grip and gently hugged him as I murmured in his ear.

"Yes. I will always come when you need me. You're mine now, just as I am yours. Don't worry, little wolf. You're safe now. I will take care of you. Always."

He flinched when my hand settled over his baby bump. Gently stroking his belly, I murmured in his ear. "Have no fear. You don't know me yet, but I'm a different kind of alpha. Your pup is as much mine now as you are, Elisha. I will treasure both of you the way you deserve."

Relaxing, Elisha leaned back, tilting his face to gaze at me through drowsy eyes. And what a beautiful shade of green they were. *So that's what color your eyes are...* Like the fuzzy moss I'd seen on trees so deep in the forest the air stayed cool and damp.

Funny, I never would've thought such a hue would be so amazing. Somehow, it was completely different—and so much lovelier—in those beautiful eyes than on the grizzled trunk of an ancient tree.

We stared at each other for a long moment, so poignant my eyes stung with tears before we both slowly began to smile.

FOUR

ELISHA

For the first time in recent memory, nothing hurt as I slowly came awake. Even the bed wasn't making my skin itch and burn. In fact, it felt like I was sleeping on a cloud. A soft cloud, lovingly cradling my body. The only possible conclusion: I was dead. Heaven probably had soft beds, right?

At the idea of a heavenly cloud bed, a giggle rose from my throat. I stopped cold, picking up on a sound which normally filled me with dread—another body was breathing beside me. Someone was here. Pulse quickening, I realized the danger of Horace thinking I might be happy.

He would be positive I was cheating on him. Or stealing. Or plotting with my father. Or any of the other things he always accused me of doing.

Except.

Wait.

Horace was dead! Hadn't I felt it myself when our bond was suddenly severed? And then I'd gotten sick... too sick. *Shoot.* Then came the pain and the whole dying and everything. The last thing I remembered was my wolf urging me to hold on.

No. Wait... my wolf *wasn't* the last thing. The pounding in my heart slowed, but my pulse remained quick as I recalled more. Oh. Oh, yes. My fantastic dream with a lover so strong and caring, it was almost impossible to imagine how my brain had ever conjured something so unreal.

Maybe I was dead, and my dream lover was actually a sex angel. Were sex angels a thing? If not, they should have been. Should I open my eyes and offer to polish his halo?

Okay, I definitely wasn't dead if I was making awful sex puns. Although polishing his halo wasn't the worst euphemism I could've come up with, just saying. Maybe I was still dreaming?

If the fever dreams had morphed from scary things climbing out of my closet into sex angels and dream lovers, I wasn't altogether sure dying from aconite poisoning was a bad way to go.

Being so clear-minded sucked, though. If I was about to float away and spend my eternity lying in a cloud bed with a sex angel, then thinking was the last thing I wanted to be doing. Maybe the goddess took reviews. I would make a note to her about this one. The only brain waves active right now should have involved my dream lover.

So open your eyes, weirdo. Maybe you leveled up to a new dream, and he's waiting for you to say hello. With your tongue. I tried hard not to smile, attempting to look like I was sleeping in case someone was really with me.

Who, though? Tell yourself the truth, Elisha. You already know you're dying. Quit squeezing your eyes so tight and open them. You won't know what you're dealing with until you do.

As much as I wanted to see if my dream lover was lying

beside me, I didn't want to ruin the fantasy. No matter how many times I'd made a wish and blown dandelion pollen or crossed my fingers when I saw a shooting star, dreams didn't actually come true. At least, not in my world.

The bed moved as whoever was beside me came closer. Something ghosted over my cheekbone... the back of a hand, maybe? Afraid to trust even a gentle touch, I flinched. The breathing came closer. Not only could I hear it better, but its heat fanned over my ear the moment before my sex angel spoke.

"I know you're awake, little wolf. Why don't you open those pretty green eyes and say hello?" My heart thudded in apprehension. This was no dream lover. It was a man... an alpha. *And he's in my bed.*

My rising panic came to an abrupt halt as I became aware of a scent. *His* scent. Oh. *Wait.* Thinking back to my dream, my lover had carried this scent at the end. The dream held more, but I couldn't remember right now. It tickled at the edge of my consciousness, refusing to be pulled free.

I simply knew the scent meant nothing but good things. And not because of my dream. If it were merely a fantasy, then why did it make me feel so... safe? My wolf lifted his head in interest, licking a paw as if preparing himself for something. *Someone.* I sniffed the air, not trying to fake sleep, yet not ready to commit to opening my eyes.

His glorious scent, though... A heady combination of pine mixed with the spicy yet floral fragrance of the night-blooming cereus. My favorite flower. A true desert beauty which bloomed once a year, and then only for a single night.

My papa taught me about it while training me in my gift. His ugly little cactus with its long, limp leaves had surprised me with its secret. I'd seen it bloom a single time.

After I turned thirteen, Papa let me stay up with him to watch the cactus come to life under the moonlight. By dawn, flowers had already begun to close. By midday, they were nothing but a memory, leaving shriveled, phallic bulbs in their place.

When I started giggling at the shape of the leftovers, Papa smiled and plucked them for the compost pile. Somehow, it made sense how my sex angel—whoever he was—would smell like my favorite flower and best memory with my papa.

Speaking of my sex angel... I took a deep breath and opened my eyes before slowly turning my head to see if he was as gorgeous as I remembered. When I met his whiskey-brown gaze, my breath came out in a whoosh.

Holy moly. He was even better than I remembered.

As a smile slowly spread across his face, the corners of his eyes crinkled. "Hello again, Elisha. How much of last night do you recall?"

I didn't know whether it was the crinkles—too human a feature for any angel, of the sex type or not—or the worry I saw in his eyes. Or the heady scent that had my wolf ready to roll over and offer his belly. Or the familiar X scar of our people over his left nipple. Maybe all the above? Whatever it was, I finally accepted this very real man was not simply my dream lover, but an alpha I could trust not to hurt me. At least, my gut was telling me so, and it was never wrong.

Words fell out of my mouth before I could censor them. "You're really real and not a dream lover or a sex angel. You're an actual alpha, and... *you saved me.*" Blinking rapidly now, my brain made more connections, and my elusive lost memory clicked into place.

My voice was breathy, probably because I was completely awestruck. "You're my mate. My new alpha. Not only because you claimed me, but for real. My *true* mate, like, fated and stuff." As I sucked in another breath, my eyes widened. *"That's* why you smell so good."

He studied me before a loud laugh rumbled from his throat. "Although I like the idea of being your ultimate fantasy, I'm sorry to admit I'm a real person. And yes, I'm your mate now. I'd prefer for you to think of me as your mate rather than your alpha. I'd never planned on taking a mate, but I always swore if I did, it would be an equal partnership."

Now I was the one laughing. "Are you sure I'm not dead, and this isn't heaven? Because I'm pretty sure no alpha worth his salt would ever say something so ridiculous. Especially to an omega."

He rolled his eyes. "Then those alphas need to find new salt." He hesitated, then lifted an arm. "Is it okay if we cuddle? My wolf needs physical contact, and I want to hold you again. I didn't dare while you slept because it was bad enough to claim you without consent. I wasn't going to force any further physical contact without your knowledge."

I practically flung myself into his arms, wrapping my arms around his neck as I snuggled in close. "Okay, so maybe you're real, but now I'm starting to wonder if I should question your sanity. As for the lack of consent, consider it given, and backdate it to whatever point in time will absolve you of any guilt. You literally saved my life. But even if you hadn't, you've already treated me with more kindness than any alpha ever has."

As those impulsive words poured out of my mouth, my heart started to pound again. Calling him crazy was a good way to press the limits of said kindness.

Wrapping his arms around me, he held me tight. His gentle touch calmed me as quickly as his softly spoken words. "Easy now, little wolf. I don't know what has you quietly freaking out, but I promise you have nothing to fear with me. I know it'll take time for you to completely trust me, but for now I'd appreciate it if you'd take me at my word. And though I've claimed you, I want to wait for anything more physical than this until you feel completely safe. When you're ready, you can initiate our intimacy."

What? Who was this alpha? He wasn't going to hit me or force me into sex? And he meant every word, or my wolf would've scented the smoothest of lies. Gulping, I slowly leaned my head back to see into his eyes. "Okay. I'll try. I'm sorry I called you crazy, though. I shouldn't have been so disrespectful."

He scoffed, looking at me like I was the crazy one. "Why the hell not? I told you I want us to be equals, didn't I? True equality means you can feel free to say anything you want to me. Never mind if it's something you don't think I want to hear. I want to start our relationship off well, which means honesty, even when it's ugly."

I bit my lip as I considered his words. "Okay. Hmm. Then in the spirit of honesty, I have to say your idea sounded both totally weird and completely awesome. Also, can you tell me your name? It seems kinda slutty to be naked cuddling and bonded without knowing what to call you. It's like a country song about waking up married after getting blackout drunk."

As if startled, he barked out a laugh. "Well, damn. Then I guess you're feeling kinda awkward right about now, aren't you?" I must have been feeling braver than I thought because I giggled and shoved his chest. He merely laughed more. "I like you, little wolf. Allow me to introduce myself and give you my backstory. Let's start with my name. I'm Matthias Longclaw, but you can call me Matt. My father was the alpha here in Lucerne Valley, and I was the original heir. I left at eighteen, and apparently my Uncle Horace challenged him not long after and took over the pack."

"Did you know your uncle?" I closed my eyes, wrinkling my nose as I gave my head a quick shake. "Never mind, don't answer. I know pack law well, thanks to my father. Mostly because he was always looking for loopholes, but there's another story. So Horace must've been the younger brother, huh? It's weird to think of someone so old and mean ever being someone's little brother. He was an evil man, and except for nearly dying, I'm not sorry he's gone."

"I'm not sorry, either. I only wish I'd killed him myself." Matt attempted to lighten the mood, grinning as he booped the tip of my nose. "You wouldn't say it was hard to imagine him being a younger brother if you'd ever met my father. There's a reason I didn't stay. Jared says the pack is different now, but the people back then never did anything to make my life easier, no matter how abusive my father was. But never mind my sob story. Why am I talking about this shit? I'm sure we have plenty of better things we can discuss."

"We can start with how you claimed your uncle-in-law as your mate. Talk about some hick stuff, right there. Even for desert rats like us." Hoping to lighten the mood again, I went for the obvious joke.

It worked, and I was startled to realize I knew not from the grin on his face but because I could feel his mood. That was... kinda trippy. And also nice. I'd never noticed it with Horace. I couldn't help but wonder if it was because Matt was my true mate or because Horace was always angry, so I could never sense anything else from him. Either way, if I hadn't already felt safe with Matt, then I definitely did now.

"You're correct, dear. I hope you might begin to trust me now?"

I jerked back when he spoke, my mouth falling open in shock. "Did you just read my mind, or was I speaking my thoughts? My brothers say I do sometimes."

Winking, Matt leaned forward with a grin and kissed my cheek. "It might be fun to tease you, but I'll save it for another time. You were thinking out loud. As for the answer, your guess is as good as mine. We'd have to ask other mated pairs, both regular and fated, to know the answer. So, you have brothers?" He winced and rolled onto his back, putting his hands behind his head as he stared at the ceiling. "I really don't want to get into this now, but eventually we're going to have to decide how to handle your father. I have to challenge him for the pack because I've claimed you, you know."

Scooting closer, I curled up against him and rested my hand on his chest. "I know. I hadn't thought far enough ahead yet, but I would've gotten there eventually. If you challenge him, do you think you could save my brothers too? They're younger than me, and both of them are also omegas. Saul is twelve, and Noah's six. I don't know if our parents spaced us out on purpose, but we're all six years apart."

Matt shivered as I played with the small, so-light-it-was-barely-there patch of hair in the center of his chest. He turned his head to grin at me. "It helps to know you're legal, but now I'm feeling like a cradle robber."

"Don't. Besides... I turned nineteen a few weeks ago. I've never been completely young, though. As the oldest, I was always expected to be mature. Also, I don't think you can rob a pregnant man's cradle, just saying." I wasn't about to mention Horace, but there was no hiding my baby. His words from what I'd thought was a dream floated back to me. "Did you mean it? You'll let me keep my baby *and* claim him or her as your own?" I didn't know why I was worried when Matt had given me no reason to be.

He rolled back on his side and scooted down so we were nose to nose. "Elisha, I never say anything I don't mean." He studied me solemnly, then winked again. "Besides, we have to keep the whole desert hick thing going, don't we? I promise I'll love my little cousin-son or daughter and treat them no different than any other pups we might have in the future."

We both laughed at the whole cousin angle. *Yeah...* we were totally going to be a unique family. Matt silenced my giggles with a toe-curling kiss. Once I started to get lost in it, he pulled back with a wistful smile.

"As much as I would love to continue, let's finish our conversation. I need to decide how to handle your father before he hears about us through the grapevine. Dealing with it head-on is the best option. No offense, but Montgomery Whitetail doesn't have a great reputation, from what I recall. And I don't want to cause you pain, but he did leave you here to die. I can't ignore or easily forgive his actions."

Thinking of my father turned my stomach. It hadn't surprised me when he hadn't produced a backup mate after killing my alpha. Shaking my head, I released a bone-deep sigh.

"Like I said, I only want you to save my brothers. The rumors aren't wrong. My father is every bit as evil as Horace was. And if he didn't save me, it was because he couldn't find anyone willing to pay a dowry or make a connection for a used, pregnant omega. I wonder if I should be offended? Considering the company he keeps, you'd think one of his nasty old friends who used to watch me like pervs would've been willing to pay something for me. They wouldn't have let me keep my baby, but I can think of one or two who might've been interested in used goods."

"Never call yourself something so awful, even if you're joking. You could never be used goods." As he growled, Matt's eyes flashed gold. "If any of those filthy old lechers ever cross our path, feel free to point them out."

A warm glow spread through me at his possessive tone. *And the growl.* His growl was totally hot. Disgust filtered through our bond at the idea of some gross old man putting his hands on me. Feeling so much closer to him already, I lifted a hand to his cheek.

"I'll keep your notes in mind. But let's go back to my father, hmm? When Horace grabbed me, I was being escorted to what was supposed to be my new home. My father had struck a deal with the alpha in Kingman, Arizona. They were solidifying their plans to steal from the government. If he'd become my mate, he and my father would've become equal partners. When there's gold and other precious minerals involved, it's hard to trust your coworkers. My father figured sweetening the deal with his virgin omega son would kill two birds with one stone. They would have a permanent connection between the packs, and he wouldn't be able to turn on his co-conspirator if it was the father of his own mate. Or something similar. Zoning out a lot was easier than thinking about the future I had in store."

"Wait. I'm gonna need you to back up. What do you mean by stealing from the government? What kind of partnership was your father offering the Arizona alpha?"

I slapped my palm against my forehead. "Sorry, I got ahead of myself. I've grown up hearing my father's schemes and watching him create his vast maze of tunnels. I guess I forgot it's not common knowledge, and you're not psychic.

Anyway. As you know, Newberry Springs is immediately outside Death Valley. Are you aware Death Valley is a national park? Sorry if I sound condescending, but you'd be surprised by how many people don't know."

"Ha! You don't sound condescending at all because I'd almost forgotten until you mentioned it. Now you have, I definitely remember because my father charged Newberry Springs a tariff whenever they wanted to pass through our territory with cross-country shipments of Borax and other minerals your pack mines to support itself." He looked thoughtful, lifting his head to brace it on his palm while he waited for me to continue.

"*Minerals* is one word for it. At least, those are what we openly mine and sell." I stretched fully on my side, mirroring his position as I faced him. "So here's the big secret. There's a lot of gold and copper, among other precious metals, to be found in Death Valley. Since he can't do it openly, given its national park status, my father has been building a series of tunnels stretching beneath it for as long as I can remember. He has a whole underground town down there where the workers live for their two-week shifts. He rotates them out every couple of weeks with replacements from the pack. Every man and boy old enough to work takes a turn down there. They started mining gold a few years ago and slipping it into the mineral shipments. The problem is the risks of getting caught are too high."

"You think?" Matt snorted.

I shrugged. "For a criminal mastermind, my father isn't the smartest guy. *Anyway*. When he finally tunneled through to the Arizona side, he started looking for my future mate. He's already using it, but carefully and under the cover of night with small vehicles. Nothing like the kind of trucks he wants to run out of there. The Kingman alpha doesn't know the location of the tunnel on his side. He was supposed to get it once we were mated."

Matt's eyes nearly bulged out of his head. "How big of trucks does he need? Surely he's not getting enough gold and copper. If so, the government might start to notice something going on at some point. Like, when the ground starts caving in? I'm mostly joking, but also not really. Any kind of mining will take a toll on the land. Isn't he worried?"

I snickered at what he must be picturing. "If you're picturing truckloads of gold, my bad. Sorry, I forgot a common mineral there he can truck in bulk. Salt. He's got a lot to unload from all the tunneling. I have no idea how much has been mined in precious metals. My father doesn't trust anyone with the full picture of his operation. I imagine he rotates the workers so often to keep them in the dark."

"This is fascinating. I never would've imagined your father, or anyone, for that matter, having the balls to build an operation right under protected government lands." His eyebrows drew together, forming the cutest crease in between as he frowned. "I wonder if he took all the men from this pack to work there? I would understand him challenging Horace for stealing you, but hearing this, it was a risky move, if for no other reason than keeping a low profile with the Supreme Council. In order to take the pack, he would've had to place an official challenge with the Territory Chief."

"Yeah, and it's dodgier than you'd think because TC Ash Woodlawn doesn't like my father. But you see, he's always talked about taking over this pack anyway. This gave him an excuse. He's been sick of paying tariffs to Horace for years now. Plus, having a secondary settlement for the top-dwelling pack members would be a good thing. We can't have too many and keep a low profile in Newberry Springs.

It's already a small town, you know? Even living out in the desert as we do, too many new faces get noticed."

Matt snorted as he raised an eyebrow. "I'm sorry, *top dwelling*?"

Vigorously nodding, I rushed to explain. "Our pack is made up of desert survivalists who are used to the heat. But some aren't as fond of the sun and actually like living in the underground town serving the tunnels. The people who live and work down there don't know any details about the mining. They cook and clean for the workers. As long as they don't get too nosy, my father lets them stay down below where it's cooler."

Lifting an arm, Matt snaked it around my waist and pulled me closer. "So basically, your father didn't kill Horace in retaliation for you. He did it to enslave my pack and take our land, not to mention save himself money in the process. You'll have to forgive me, but any reservations I had about taking him out are gone. After he abandoned you to your fate, I was already fighting my wolf anyway. But now? He's going down."

Pressing a kiss against his shoulder, I turned my face into his neck where his scent was strongest. "My father was never kind to me, Matt. I was nothing but another one of his commodities. Do to him what you will, but please save my brothers."

FIVE

MATT

After spending the morning in bed cuddling and talking things through with Elisha, I felt much better about everything. I wasn't proud of forcing a claim, but his forgiveness and instant acceptance went a long way to soothe my battered soul.

Not to mention knowing I'd had no other choice. Even though I'd been gentle and treated him with respect, part of me hadn't been able to see my actions as anything other than unforgivable.

When Elisha fretted about the state of his kitchen after being out of it for so long, we finally forced ourselves to dress and head downstairs. Jared was waiting at the bottom of the stairs with a tight smile and concern etched in the corners of his eyes.

My wolf was immediately on alert. "Is everything all right, Jared? Neat trick, by the way. How did you know we were coming? Are you psychic, or do you have bat ears?"

At my teasing, Jared blinked a couple times before relaxing and dishing some back. "As your beta, being somewhat psychic is my job so I can anticipate your every need."

He winked almost stoically before turning to Elisha with a grin. "It's good to see you up and around again, Alpha Mate. And looking so refreshed, might I say. Let me guess, you came down to make sure no one ruined your kitchen or garden in your absence?"

Blushing, Elisha looked down as he nodded. "I keep telling you the formal title isn't necessary when we're alone, Jared. Stop it before I forget your name and start calling you Beta." Lifting his head, Elisha grinned shyly and rubbed his cheek against my arm, marking me as he would in animal form. "Thank you for finding Matt. He told me you called and asked him to come. I owe you a debt I can never repay. Surely we're on a first-name basis."

"I'll do my best to use your name, Elisha. For the record, you don't owe me a thing. It was my pleasure, and, truth be told, I was selfishly happy to have an excuse to get Matt to come home." As we headed down the hallway toward the kitchen, he fell into step with us. "Matt, I hate to do this to you, but the reason you found me expecting you is because I was watching for you. The Gamma Council is waiting in the war room. We need to officially accept you as Alpha and take care of pack business."

That got my attention. "Has there been word from Elisha's father?"

"Not yet. But I assume he'll be checking on Elisha sooner than later, and I need to know how to respond when he calls." With one simple comment, Jared's pinched look was back.

Elisha huffed a half-laugh. "Don't hold your breath, Jared. My father is more concerned with acclimating the new men into the pack than he is about anything which may or may not have happened to me. He did take our men, right? The last few days are kind of fuzzy, but I recall hearing something about my home pack coming here. And there was a fight, wasn't there?"

"Unfortunately, you are remembering correctly." Jared sighed, shaking his head. "Aside from the Gamma Council and their families who were here at the time of the attack, Newberry Springs took every man and boy old enough to work."

Showing himself the perfect Alpha Mate, Elisha stopped midstep and clutched Jared's arm. "All those families were torn apart? As if their lives weren't hard enough already. How many remain? And I'm assuming they're still without power in town, aren't we? We need to make sure our people have food. I've got to get out to the garden. I'm certain I have plenty of vegetables ready for harvesting."

I slipped an arm around my mate, pressing a kiss to the top of his head, while Jared rushed to answer him. "Don't worry, Elisha. Matt had me bring all thirty-one remaining pack members here to the manse. I put them in the third-floor dorms, across from the infirmary. There was plenty of room in the Delta quarters anyway, and the only deltas we have are in the infirmary. So it was an easy answer."

Before I could, Elisha asked the obvious question, proving once again how invested he was in this pack. "How many wounded deltas are being treated? And do we have enough supplies for the healer?"

"We had seventeen wounded deeper than a simple shift would cure. Obviously, Newberry Springs took the ones with the lightest injuries. And yes, I think Isaac has everything he needs, or he would've been in my face about it already." Jared and Elisha shared a smile, telling me our current epsilon must have been a force to be reckoned with. I wasn't surprised. I'd always found quirkiness a common trait in epsilons.

Elisha muttered soundlessly, his lips moving as if doing mental math, and glanced at Jared. "Thirty-one pack members, seventeen injured, and then we have the gamma families, which accounts for another twenty-three people, if I'm remembering correctly. And with the eleven normal residents, we have eighty-two mouths to feed. Has a service roster been put in place to have our guests help out? The staff must be losing their minds."

At Jared's crestfallen look, I stifled a laugh. "Forgive me, Elisha. I hadn't thought so far ahead. The pack moved in yesterday, but that's no excuse. Especially when the gamma families have been here for three days. No wonder my mother served me cold tea and a stony glare with my breakfast. I will add it to my to-do list at once."

"There is no need. I'm on it, and you have enough on your plate, Jared. I just wanted to know what I'm walking into when I go through the kitchen doors. You know I like to take charge of the manse. By the time you finish your meeting, I'll have everything running like clockwork." Smiling gently, Elisha gave Jared an encouraging pat on the shoulder. "Come find me later, and I'll make sure you get a hot cup of tea. I'll also let Paula know how hard you've been working."

Jared's eyes went wide with alarm. "You don't have to stick up for me with my mom. She was simply worried about you, and then the extra cooking and cleaning probably didn't help." He looked around before lowering his voice. "As you can imagine, the gamma families are above offering to pitch in." I smothered a smile, knowing damn well what he meant. Since the gammas always made up the pack council, their mates and children acted like they were better than everyone else.

Snorting, Elisha was already shaking his head. "Well,

their poopy behavior won't fly. I'll lead by example and have them helping me weed the garden and harvest the veggies. The first one who cries without breaking a nail gets transferred to maid detail. Don't worry. I'll have this household running like a top again shortly."

As if second-guessing himself, he paused and turned to smile almost timidly at me. "Is it okay if I drop your name if necessary? Most pack members will respect my position, but there are always those who need to know the alpha supports me. It goes double for gamma mates."

I bent to give him a quick kiss. "Drop my title all you want, sweetheart. And I'll ask you for the names of anyone who needed mine. I wanted to invite you to the meeting, to show the council I intend for us to rule as a pair. After hearing everything you've had to say, I'm completely certain I want us to be viewed as equals. I wouldn't want anything less, especially for my true mate. It needs to be clear from the start: we are two halves of a whole."

Resting a hand on my chest, Elisha smiled so sweetly my wolf was rolling around inside me, baring his belly for our mate. And I was right there with him. The trust and affection flowing through the bond was enough to bring me to my knees. Staying upright and remembering to hold myself together and behave like an alpha took all I had. I'm not sure what he sensed through our bond, but Elisha's eyes twinkled as he shook his head.

"Thank you, Matt. And maybe later I'll want to go to one of your meetings, but at the moment, I need to get the household in line. Even if we'll be ruling together, we still have our separate jobs and duties. I get to worry about the needs of the pack while you have to think first of their safety. Also? Please don't feel you have to include me in any biting ceremonies. I would prefer to be the guy taking the pictures, thank you very much. And remember to go easy on them if the pack takes time to accept you giving me equal power."

All I could do was stare at him. How could someone so young be so wise and self-possessed? Swallowing a lump in my throat, I brushed my fingers over his cheek. "You humble me, Elisha. I can see already you're going to make me a better alpha. Okay. I'll let you take care of your business while I go tend to mine. We can fill each other in later on anything important."

"I like your idea. I'm going to have to think about it, but I'll find a time in our schedules for us to have private conversation about pack matters and anything else that might come up." He waggled his brows with the word *up*, and his cheeks flushed pink, my sole clue he intended it as innuendo. Hot damn, I really did win the lottery in the mate department. Elisha giggled to himself and rushed off to the kitchen doors, leaving me alone with Jared.

Jared looked befuddled before getting back to business. He tilted his chin toward a hallway veering off to the right. "True mates, huh? Now I'm doubly glad about calling you home. Let's get to the war room. The Gamma Council meets in the conference room across from your father's old office. Horace didn't like the lighting in there, so he kept a desk in the war room. Personally, I think he was afraid the gammas might secretly meet and vote to overthrow him. There's always another alpha to be found if a pack is desperate enough."

"It sounds like my uncle didn't trust anyone. Based on what's left of our town, I can see why. You don't get to treat your people like shit and then expect them to respect you. Fear you, sure. But true respect comes from trust, and it has to be earned." Jerking my head from side to side, I stretched my neck and took a deep breath as we approached the door to the war room. "Okay, Jared. Here goes nothing. Let's see if the gammas are willing to give me a chance to show them I can be a better alpha than my father and uncle."

"Don't worry about it, Matt. Anyone who spends three minutes with you will see you are nothing like our two former alphas." He patted my shoulder, then opened the door and led me into the room. I recognized every last one of the four gamma wolves sitting around the table. If I hadn't gone to school with them, I knew of them through one of their younger siblings or from town. Jared was right; the pack was much younger now, and our generation had stepped up to the plate.

Although, since two of these men had bullied me when we were kids, my immediate acceptance of alpha wasn't guaranteed. Especially since I hadn't challenged Monty yet. This was gonna be fun. Straightening my shoulders, I held myself to my full height and let them feel the weight of my alpha pheromones while Jared introduced me.

"Sorry to keep you waiting, gentlemen. As a newly mated alpha, I'm sure you will understand Alpha Matthias wasn't available as early as we'd hoped. He's here now, and I formally petition as pack beta for the immediate acceptance of Matthias Longclaw as the new alpha of the Lucerne Valley pack. Do I hear a second to my petition?"

Marcus Favre, another old friend from childhood, rose to his feet. "I second the petition."

As officious as I'd ever seen him, Jared nodded and looked around the table. "Do I have a third, or does someone have another petition they wish to nominate for consideration?"

I was surprised when Bradley Shaw, a guy who'd kicked my ass more times than I cared to remember, was the next to stand. "I'm happy to back you up as third. Matty Longclaw is one of us, and I know he will do what's right by Lucerne Valley."

"We have the two support votes needed to secure my petition. Are there any objections? Bear in mind our pack was Matthias' birthright. He left to escape the same brutish behavior we all witnessed with our last two alphas. Not only did he come back to a pack who failed to support him as a pup living in an abusive home, but he has already claimed our Alpha Mate Elisha. Furthermore, Elisha is his true mate, which means the fates have had a hand in bringing both of them here."

While they digested his statement, everyone was quiet. Jared opened his mouth as if to move on, but a nerdy guy with thick glasses and a shapeless mop of hair slowly raised a trembling hand. "I think I want to raise an objection."

More than one person in the room rolled their eyes. Jared looked mildly irritated but managed to sound patient. "You *think* you want to object? I'm sorry, Fredo. I'm going to need more information before I can accept. Especially since you're uncertain whether you even want to make it in the first place."

Fredo sat up straighter. "Forgive me, but I have to question why someone who would run away rather than accept his birthright of alpha heir should automatically be up for petition. Also, the previous Longclaw alphas put their own needs ahead of the pack. How do we know this one will be any different?"

When Jared looked ready to jump to my defense, I touched him on the arm. "Jared, if I might be given a chance to speak on my own behalf, I think I can answer Fredo's concerns."

Nodding, Jared motioned for me to speak. The little

sneak made sure to toss in what he already considered my official title. "Very well, Alpha Matthias. You may have the floor."

Glancing around at the two seated men and the two standing, I stepped forward and pulled out a chair. "First, can we please be less formal? Come on, guys, it's me. We don't need to stand on ceremony to have this discussion and vote."

Grinning, Marcus sat down first. "I accept. Informal for the win."

Bradley took a seat and gestured toward my chair. "By all means, sit down, and let's talk this out, Matty."

I pulled out a second chair, waiting for Jared to reluctantly accept informality, though it was obviously rubbing him wrong, based on his gritted teeth and pinched expression. "Good man. Thank you." I patted Jared on the shoulder and finally took my own seat.

Looking around the long table, I took a deep breath while gathering my thoughts. "First off, I don't know what happened during my own uncle's time as your alpha. Based on what I saw when I rode through town, it wasn't anything good. As for my father? He did put the pack first, so I'll beg to differ with you, Fredo."

Chuckling humorlessly, I drummed my fingers on the table top. "My father put the pack first at all times. When I was growing up, we lacked for nothing. The only one he didn't make time for was me, unless it was to beat, belittle, or berate me for one imagined flaw or another. You want to know why I left? I didn't want to be like my father or with a pack who accepted his kind of toxicity as acceptable behavior."

Fredo winced apologetically. "Forgive me. I was unaware of your personal history. May I ask why you returned? We know what Jared has reported, but I'd like to hear it from you. No offense, but we don't know where you've been for the past ten years."

"Fair," I said agreeably, holding my palms up for good measure. "I knocked around a little at first, staying with my grandparents off and on after they moved, but mostly spending my time traveling and exploring the wider world. Along the way, I met four displaced alpha sons who quickly became like family to me. The five of us eventually formed a motorcycle club, basically a small alpha-only pack. We call ourselves the West Coast Wolves and spend our days traveling the roads and helping anyone we find in need."

Shawn Elderberry—a guy I remembered as both outgoing and argumentative as hell—looked fascinated as he leaned forward with his forearms resting on the table. "Seriously? Five alphas formed a pack and didn't kill each other? And the Supreme Council allowed it?"

Playfully wagging a finger, I tutted in response. "Ah, ah, ah. You're forgetting something, Shawn. The Supreme Council only gets a say with official sanctioned packs. But for the record? The one alpha per pack rule is tradition, not law. You should probably know before you vote—I have no intentions of ever turning any of my children out at eighteen if I have more than one alpha son. If you ask me, it breeds resentment between siblings who should be close."

Fredo held his hand up again. "I've heard enough to withdraw any objection I may have had. Even if you didn't get to answer why you came back."

I shrugged. "Isn't it obvious? I told you I spend my days helping people in need. When Jared told me Elisha was dying of aconite poisoning, what choice did I have? Fortunately, Elisha has forgiven me for claiming him without clear consent. And yes, we were blessed to find we are true mates. Still, coming here to claim a delirious dying man wasn't easy for me to do. But I did it—true mate or not—because it was the right thing. Isn't it funny how you have to vote to accept me, but Horace and Monty both seized Lucerne Valley by killing the sitting alpha in a challenge?"

Jared favored me with a respectful smile. "And yet you saved him anyway. Knowing you might not get anything out of it other than a mate who you'd be responsible for from now on, you came. You also knew you will most likely have to kill your mate's father to regain control of the pack. And our tactic is to make you explain yourself while we decide how to place a vote no one should bother questioning." As if he smelled a fart, his nostrils flared. "Unless there are any further objections, I suggest we vote so we can move on with our meeting. All in favor of Matthias Longclaw taking over as our pack's chosen alpha, say aye."

All five members of the council, including Jared, assented in unison, raising their hands for good measure. Huffing a loud breath, Jared nodded his approval. "Very good. Alpha Matthias, do you accept the position being offered? Not because it's your birthright or because you claimed our former Alpha Mate, but because all five of us have spoken as one and chosen you to be our leader."

I couldn't help it—I teared up at his words. After swallowing an inconvenient lump in my throat, I nodded with every bit of solemnity the occasion called for. "I do accept. And quite humbly, might I add. I appreciate each of you putting your trust in me, and I'll do my best to prove I deserve it."

As my head spun, they all rose and walked around to form a line behind me, taking a knee and extending their left wrists. Jared claimed center position with two gammas on either side of him—an official council formation I hadn't seen in so long I'd forgotten about it. Staring me straight in the eye, Jared nearly had me tearing up all over again. "Alpha Matthias, we the governing Council of the Lucerne Valley Pack are ready to swear our allegiance to you completely."

Pushing my chair back, I stood and took a deep breath as I prepared to accept their allegiance. Since the pack bond would've magically transferred to Monty at the moment Horace died, he would feel a break in the communal link when I claimed them as my pack. And he'd know what it meant, too. While I'd never experienced it firsthand, during a lifetime of learning at my father's feet, I'd both seen and heard his reactions when pack members either died or left and swore allegiance to another. Apparently, one brought a feeling of loss and grief, while the other simply clicked off like a light switch.

I wouldn't know until I felt it myself for the first time, but at least I knew I could expect to hear from Monty by the end of the day.

It was such a simple act, but so humbling to bend over and bite the extended wrist. I started on the left end with Fredo. My laniary fangs dropped into position behind my canines, but this time, no poison would be delivered. My saliva mixing with their blood would form the pack bond. I hesitated for no more than a second before biting down over the fading scar from my uncle's bite. It would have begun to disappear at the moment of his death, when a new alpha took over the pack. If Monty wanted to retain the pack past a full lunar cycle after the previous alpha's death, he would've needed to demand their allegiance with a bite of his own.

His failure to come here to personally claim the remaining pack and its gammas showed his cowardice.

Without asking, I knew the fucker had been waiting for Elisha to die before completely asserting himself in Lucerne Valley. Thinking about him pissed me off, so I pushed it to the back of my mind and focused on this momentous occasion I'd never expected to experience.

As soon as my teeth broke Fredo's flesh, the sweetness of his blood burst on my tongue. The bond clicked instantly into place, cementing when I licked the wrist to hasten the healing of the scar. I did the same to Shawn, feeling awe as a new family member joined my pack consciousness. Before I bit Jared's wrist, he and I shared a smile and a nod. Then I moved on to Bradley and Marcus.

Jared held up his freshly healing scar, smiling as he pointed out how Horace's bite had already been completely erased by mine. I wasn't sure what to say, so I nodded toward the table. "Okay, since we have taken care of that bit of business, everyone get settled in so you can tell me why the hell our town looks like shit before we start discussing the Monty situation."

As they filled me in on how badly things were thanks to my uncle's shoddy and self-centered leadership, I got pissed off all over again. I thought about the freshly decorated guest suite I'd commandeered last night. A room set aside on the off chance our Territory Chief might come visit and want to spend a night. Meanwhile, the town crumbled around him. This fancy alpha manse had green lawns and Wi-Fi, while the community park was overgrown with weeds.

"What's up with the electricity situation? I didn't see one light when I went through town last night. Is the pack so broke we can't afford to leave security lights on in the stores anymore? Honestly, it looked like a ghost town."

Disgusted, Shawn waved a hand toward the recessed

lighting over our heads. "Horace had solar power installed here a few years ago. A few months later, a killer storm went through, and a bolt of lightning knocked out the transformer providing power to the town. He refused to report it or allow us to repair it ourselves because he didn't trust humans enough to call the power company."

I nearly choked on my tongue. "Seriously? How did people stay in business? Did he not charge them the same taxes my father did? Sorry, I'm trying to understand why he wouldn't care enough to make sure the pack had power."

Jared tapped his finger rapidly against the table, the sole sign of stress on his otherwise placid demeanor. "No, it was quite the opposite, in fact. Horace raised pack taxes, but he did nothing in exchange. The few businesses still operational used generators to get by. I've been trying to convince the pack to combine their resources for solar power or even a few wind-powered turbines, but no dice. It's hard to argue when the business owners counter with how much they are already paying in taxes."

Growling softly, Shawn narrowed his eyes. "They're right. Why should they provide their own utilities when they pay taxes to the pack? We were about to force the issue at our next council meeting, but Horace was killed. It's not simply the electricity—it's everything. Road maintenance, waste removal, and pretty much anything else you can think of. When the town well ran low, we had to let the community garden die. We need to drill for another one. But again, it was part of a long list of things needing to be done for the pack."

What I heard disgusted me, and I felt guilty for never checking back over the years to see how my pack was faring. If I had, I would've known how bad things had gotten and dealt with my uncle myself. Even while silently vowing the pack would never go without again, I couldn't help but ask the obvious question.

"Forgive me if this is offensive, but what about you guys? Isn't the whole purpose of having a gamma council supposed to be a safeguard to make sure people like my uncle don't mistreat their pack?"

Marcus shrugged. "One would think, but not in this case. Horace cited old laws stating our purpose is for pack protection when it comes to overseeing the deltas and planning for defensive maneuvers."

Jared touched my hand. "I reached out to Territory Chief Woodlawn and made an appointment with his office more than once. I wanted him to come visit and see things for himself, but every time, he would cancel my appointment and call Horace instead. He took Horace at his word, and we got left to struggle on our own. After Horace threatened to remove me from my position and kick me out of the pack, I stopped trying."

Now I was pissed off all over again. "Is TC Woodlawn part of the good old boy system or what? I have half a mind to take pictures and send a report to the Supreme Council over this because he failed you."

Bradley held his palms up. "I've met TC Woodlawn, and he's not really a bad guy. Honestly? I think those LA packs and their constant fighting take most of his attention. And what doesn't go to them gets pulled by the water crisis in the central valley or those pretentious mofos in the Bay Area who always claim Southern California gets all the attention. He screwed up where we're concerned, don't get me wrong. I'm just saying I don't think it was intentional."

"Okay, let's table the rest for another day." I took a deep breath, knowing they might be resistant to my first order of business, but my gut said it was the right call. "These are my immediate plans, so you know where I'm at. The small pack of alphas I told you about? I'm going to call them and ask for their assistance."

Staring at me in alarm, Fredo whipped his glasses off, wiping them on his shirt. "I'm not questioning you, Alpha Matthias. Do you think having a group of strange alphas here with everything else already going on is wise? I understand you're friends with them, but surely you can see why I might have cause to be concerned."

I nodded to acknowledge his fears. "I get it, Fredo. But you can trust me when I promise these alphas are different. If anything, seeing us together might break a few stereotypes about whether or not alphas can peacefully coexist. In all our years, none of us ever felt the need to be in charge of our MC. We voted democratically on anything important. Equal voices all around, believe it or not."

He put his glasses back on, thankfully a little less nervous. "If you say so, then I will take your word for it."

"Thank you. I appreciate your trust. And by the way? I'm not one to stand on formality. This Alpha Matthias shit has to go. Unless we're doing something requiring titles, I'd prefer it if you all called me Matt. That being said, let me explain why I'm calling my buddies in. With all of our deltas and able-bodied men taken to Newberry Springs, we're sitting ducks for Monty or any other Alpha to show up and try to take over. I'm not looking for all-out war, but I will not allow members of this pack to be enslaved."

Since they all seemed shocked, I nodded confidently. "Elisha shared some interesting information about an illegal mining operation Monty is running right under the government's noses. Make no mistake, he didn't take our men to beef up his security. He wanted fresh backs he could put to work. I'm not sure if you're aware, although I would hope you are, but the moment you swore your allegiance to me, Monty would've felt the loss. And since I plan to claim the rest of the pack present today, he will know for sure another Alpha has come to Lucerne Valley."

Jared held his hands up with a rueful grin. "I knew, yes. I suppose I was hoping you would be able to handle it if he shows up."

When I playfully flipped Jared off, everyone laughed. "Way to throw me under the bus, buddy. Seriously, though, I don't expect him to show up here. He's the type to gather his information before he strikes. And since he knows I don't have any delta fighters, he won't be worried when I extend an official challenge. Nobody would ever expect me to show up with a pack of alphas as backup. Hence why I need my buddies' assistance. With them, I feel confident I can handle a challenge with the dirtiest fighter. Afterwards, you have my word—fixing our town will be my next priority. Any questions?"

"One from me." Jared pulled out his phone and started tapping. "Do you want to greet the pack in the ballroom or out on the lawn? You heard Elisha earlier—we have eighty-two people, counting yourself. Subtracting the six of us and Elisha leaves seventy-five pack members for you to meet, if not claim."

I started asking why I wouldn't be claiming everyone, until I remembered the children. Thank fuck kids under eighteen were automatically linked to their Alpha through their parents. I wouldn't have to bite any babies. "I haven't checked the weather. My answer depends on whether it's under or over ninety today."

Eyes crinkling with laughter, Jared glanced up. "It's exactly ninety degrees in the shade. Ballroom?"

"You even have to ask? Also, let's lose the whole ballroom thing. We aren't a fancy pack. Call it the party room or something, but let's not pretend we're bougey enough up in here for a damned ballroom."

The meeting ended, and we went our separate ways while I called Tucker. By the time I got off the phone with his nosy ass, I had their word: the West Coast Wolves would be here tomorrow morning. They would've come sooner, but they'd headed upstate this morning and would have to circle back. Tucker tried to give me shit about making them waste fuel, but I didn't buy it. They should've known I would be calling. The way I saw it, it was on them for not thinking ahead and already camping out somewhere nearby.

Jared had everyone in the ballroom when I arrived with Elisha at my side. Oh, yeah... meeting up with my mate for an update and a few kisses had been a necessity beforehand.

After Jared and a firmly united gamma council introduced me, the pack seemed willing to accept my leadership. I held Elisha's hand and prepared to give a short but impassioned speech. Looking around at the familiar faces sprinkled among the new but equally friendly ones, my chest swelled with the need to protect these people. This pack. My pack.

"I'm going to keep this short and sweet because I believe actions speak louder than words. As Beta Jared told you, he and the entire Gamma Council have already sworn their allegiance to me. They did for the same reason I'm going to ask you to consider it. While I was born alpha heir to this pack, I walked away from my birthright because I didn't want to become my father. You can double that for my uncle. I'm nothing like either of those men, and you can feel free to kill me in my sleep if I ever show signs."

More than a few chuckles sounded, and I could feel the

acceptance flowing around me. "If you accept me as your Alpha, do it because you want fair leadership. Not because I saved Alpha Mate Elisha or can save you from his father. Since Elisha is my true mate, believe me when I say accepting him was no hardship. I would've preferred he wasn't dying at the time, but life happens, am I right?" I paused for another wave of laughter before continuing.

"This is what you need to know. I would prefer to be called Matt. Elisha will lead this pack at my side, and I expect him to receive the same dignity and respect you would offer me. Moving forward, I'm already planning some major changes around here."

When I saw I had their attention, I nodded. "Yes, you heard me correctly. Even though I haven't been formally accepted by each of you quite yet, I'm already making plans for our future. I'm going to have Jared look into the tax situation. I feel certain you could expect them lowered. Good God, I sound like a damn politician. I don't mean to. I just wanted to put the idea out there because I heard about how heavily taxed you were under my uncle." More laughter echoed around me.

"In addition to lower taxes, I also want to return our pack to its former glory. Fixing the electricity and drilling a new well is going to take priority, and then we'll see about some community beautification projects. I want us all to take pride in Lucerne Valley again. But first, we need to bring our missing pack members home. My first official act as Alpha will be contacting our territory chief and filing an official challenge against Monty Whitetail. After I do a little homework, of course. Once our pack is united and we can move forward, I promise I'll do my best to be an Alpha you can trust to take care of your needs and provide the protection you deserve."

Turning to Elisha, I lifted a brow. "Did you have anything to add, little wolf? Maybe tell the pack how awesome I am and why they want me?"

Shrugging, Elisha managed to look completely innocent as he looked around the room. "I don't know why he's asking me. I barely know the guy. Besides, I really hope many of you would not want him for the same reasons I do. I mean, I love all of you like family, and you're my pack, but you'd better *not* be looking at my man."

He winked, and every woman in the room seemed to melt on the spot. Damn. He was born to lead and obviously fit right in here. And fuck, but if knowing my Elisha already had this pack's love and support didn't make me happy. Grinning, Elisha held up his free hand. "Everyone over eighteen who agrees this sexy man should be our pack Alpha, raise your hand."

How easily he had everyone ready to vote—and it was unanimous. Elisha blushed bright red but grinned proudly when I thanked him with a kiss on the cheek. After making a mental note to give more public displays of affection since it made my mate flush so prettily, I gave his hand a squeeze, and we went to greet our pack. Elisha hadn't been joking earlier because he pulled his phone out and took lots of pictures while I gave claiming bites to the adults and greeted the children.

By the time I was done, hope and excitement shone in the pack consciousness through our new bond. Because so many members of the pack had bonded with me, it was no surprise when Jared greeted me by the door with a smug smile, holding up his phone.

"Alpha Whitetail called to check on the pack."

Damn, he responded even faster than I'd expected. "Good. What did you tell him?"

"Exactly what you said to do before the pack meeting. I told him you were the one to speak to, and I gave him your number. Oh, and I might have also rubbed it in by telling him there was another Longclaw Alpha in Lucerne Valley. Too much?"

"Hell no. Not only was it not too much, I almost wish you'd made it worse by mentioning Elisha is my mate. The lone reason I had an opening was because he didn't care enough about his own child to find an alpha to save his life."

My phone rang, and I glanced at the screen before sending Monty's call to voicemail. *Let the fucker stew for a while.* When he saw, Elisha giggled. "You know ignoring him's going to drive him crazy, right?"

"You see the plan, little wolf. Now come on. I feel like it's been way too long since we've had us some alone time."

SIX

ELISHA

I was secretly glad Matt and I were both early risers because I had the kitchen to myself while I made breakfast.

Not completely to myself, actually. But my companion was the best part. Matt sat at the small table where Paula and I often drank tea while going over the menus for the day.

Matt looked so big on the tiny wooden chair. Though he was drinking coffee and pretending to check in with the wider world on his phone, I felt his eyes on me.

And I liked it. So did my wolf. In my mind's eye, he preened and licked his paws as if preparing to present himself to our mate.

Silly boy. This was my time. When the human got to shine.

Matt glanced up, as if sensing me thinking about him. Heck, maybe he did. I was still getting used to this whole true mate bond.

He set his phone aside and took a sip of coffee before speaking in a rumbly, early-morning growly voice, sending a shiver up my spine.

"Are you sure you don't want some help, little wolf? I can cook, you know. Get me out in the woods by a campfire, and I can whip up an Irish stew to make you cry. In a good way, I mean. Because it's... never mind. My point is I feel bad watching my pregnant mate cook while I sit on my ass."

What was it about a strong, powerful alpha tripping over his words which merely made him hotter? Grabbing the tongs, I flipped slices of bacon as I shook my head. "Being pregnant won't keep me from taking care of you. This is something I enjoy. It's why I spend so much time here."

"If you say so." He sounded doubtful but seemed willing to accept my words at face value. The way Matt listened to me was almost as amazing as an alpha offering to cook in the first place. "How did Paula take you wanting to be more involved? She's managed this household longer than I've been alive."

Stirring the scrambled eggs, I grinned over my shoulder. "It was rough at first, I can't lie. I think it was a combination of things. At first, she hated saying no when everyone knew how badly Horace treated me. I should probably be embarrassed for using my situation to my advantage, but cooking calms me, and it helped me escape at a time I needed it the most. Then she saw I knew what I was doing, and I think she's grown to like the help. Now we work as a team, and she's able to pull back."

"Good. Paula should start taking more time for herself. Especially when she has someone she can trust. And you should never feel badly for doing whatever it took to get through your ordeal with my uncle. I know you haven't told me everything, and you don't need to. Speaking of which, you've been part of this pack for the better part of six months, right? Have you spent much time in town? Because it needs a lot of attention after we are able to settle down the pack and start moving forward."

Humming, I plated our food and carried it over to the table. My heart fluttered when Matt reached over and pulled my chair out. After I gratefully sat down, I groaned, realizing I'd forgotten my juice. Dropping the napkin, I went to rise, but Matt was on his feet before I had a chance to move.

"What did you forget? Let me get it for you. You've been on your feet long enough. It's time for a break."

My heart fluttered again, and I blushed as I motioned toward my glass. "Thank you. I need my orange juice. Oh, and I buttered the toast, but there's apricot preserves in the fridge, if you want some. I canned them myself last month, so I can vouch for their yumminess factor."

"Homemade apricot preserves? Yes, please." Matt snagged the jar out of the fridge before setting both items on the table. I waited until he sat down to answer his question.

"Back to the topic of the town, yes, I'm aware of how much needs to be done. There are a lot of abandoned homes also. From what I've heard, over half the pack have moved on in recent years. Between Horace's bad temper and poor management and how hard it is to live in the desert anyway, a lot of people petitioned for transfers to packs up north or back east."

"Really? I'm not surprised. I wonder if those homes are habitable? Sounds like something I should put on my ever-growing to-do list."

Nodding, I swallowed the bite in my mouth. "It's why I brought it up. It occurred to me how after you challenge my father, you will be in the same position as he is right now—

an alpha with two packs to either merge or manage. A lot of the people in Newberry Springs seemed to be happy enough where they are. But if you give them the option, I know of at least a dozen families who would jump at the opportunity to settle in here at Lucerne Valley. It would be good if we had houses for them."

"Good idea. I hadn't thought about taking on a second pack. I'm sure I would've got there eventually, but I've been a bit preoccupied over the last couple days. If memory serves, the pack members can choose to rent or buy their home from us. When they leave, they have to sell it back to the pack for current market value. Which means we own those houses, don't we?"

"Yes, you understand exactly how it works. So we need to take responsibility for fixing up the empty houses before they can be rented. If people want to buy them as-is, they can pick them up themselves and still save money on the property. I know it's early days to discuss this, but it's definitely something to keep in mind."

Matt dangled a slice of bacon in front of me, playfully bouncing it up and down until I nipped at it. For half a second, I thought he was going to play keep-away, but he surprised me with a satisfied smile, as if feeding me pleased him. Then he winked and popped the rest into his own mouth. He finished chewing and took a swig of coffee before continuing our conversation.

"Yes and no on the whole early days thing. It's crazy how time will fly before we know it. Best to have a plan in place, especially with so much to be done. I asked Jared to look into the cost differences between wind turbines and going solar. Given our unique location, wind and sunshine are both plentiful. There's always the option of getting the power fixed, but I like the idea of being off the grid and remaining self-sufficient. Not because I'm afraid to have humans around—quite the opposite. They're welcome to come, for all I care. But I'd be interested in saving money for the pack, and paying for power we could get for free isn't going to accomplish my goal."

Being appreciated by an alpha and included in his planning felt so good. I was still surprised by how modern Matt was, but having him treat me like an equal was mind-blowing. I'd never known an alpha could possibly be so open-minded and fair. Rubbing my belly, I couldn't help but thank my lucky stars for Matt.

Any other alpha would've been within their rights to cut my pup right from my belly and force me to shift and heal so they could impregnate me themself. Instead, Matt told me he would love this pup as much as any future children. It could've been because we were true mates, but I didn't think so. Matt was simply that decent; I was sure of it.

Thinking of how he'd introduced me to the pack as his equal was as crazy as hearing him say it in the first place. With his fairness in mind, I decided to bring up a crazy idea I'd had for a while now.

"You don't mind having humans around? Good. This is something way long-term down the road on the idea list, but the Calico Ghost Town does excellent business. Not too long after I arrived, Horace was tied up with the Gamma Council, and Jared took me on a tour of our pack lands. There's a strip of old buildings off the highway near Barstow. It would make a cute tourist trap. Having the place rotting away out there in the middle of the desert when we could be earning pack revenue and retaining local history at the same time seems like such a waste."

As if trying to place the area, Matt frowned. It only took a few seconds before a bright smile crossed his face. "Rio de Oro! Or as it later came to be called, Gold River. The original settlers arrived with some Mexican miners who swore a vein of gold flowed through the desert as thick as a river. It's another victim of the gold rush era, I'm afraid. I like your idea, though. I can see where it could work. Plus, our people will need jobs once things get back to normal. A renovation would be a good project to consider. We'll bring it up at the next gamma council meeting, see if we can't find support for your idea."

"Really? You would?"

"Of course. But I won't have to because you will. Remember the whole 'us being equals' thing? I want you at future council meetings so you're informed and can have a voice on things we discuss. I plan to go back to the old way of having the pack run more democratically, with a council weighing in and us overseeing it all. Too much power isn't good for anyone, and I don't need the enticement."

He shot me a wry grin, but I wasn't buying it. No way would Matt be tempted like other alphas. He'd already proven as much by thinking of ways to limit his reach in the first place. Horace wouldn't even have considered it.

Rubbing my belly again, I smiled back at my handsome mate. Yep... I was one lucky omega, and this was a very fortunate pack to have Matt as our Alpha.

We were finishing breakfast when the house woke up. First Jared, then Paula, joined us in the kitchen. Jared was looking for Matt, and Paula was eager to start planning our day. Matt gave my hand a squeeze, regretful we would have to separate to our different tasks.

He leaned over as if about to kiss me goodbye when I jerked with an unmanly squeak at the rumble of motorcycles. Pausing, Matt tilted his head as if listening to the engines, and a wide smile spread from cheek to cheek.

"Hold that thought, little wolf. You can come back to work in a few. First, I have some friends I'd like you to meet."

SEVEN

MATT

I'm not sure who was more startled, Elisha or Jared or maybe even Paula, when I lifted Elisha in my arms and backed through the swinging kitchen door before taking off at a run. While I whooped with laughter, Elisha froze, then burst out in a joyous giggle, making me glad I'd followed my spontaneous urge.

As I stopped to open the front door, Elisha laughed in my ear. "You're crazy. Put me down. I must weigh a ton."

"A ton? I hardly think so, unless you measure your weight by sweetness factor." I stopped to sneak a quick kiss before flinging the door open and walking out onto the porch. "Sweetheart, I've carried wet dogs heavier than you. And if you're picturing a Yorkie, you'd be correct."

Giggling again, he smacked my chest. "I was joking before, but now I'm begging you. Put me down so I can pretend we're civilized when I meet your friends."

"Elisha, these guys are my brothers. They know damn well I'm not civilized. I'm counting on you to make me look good." Chuckling, I set him back on his feet right as four familiar bikes rolled to a stop. Catching Elisha by the hand, I kept him firmly at my side while we walked down the few steps to meet them.

Lucian had removed his helmet, walking our way before anyone else was off their bike. Whistling, he waved a hand in front of his face, waggling his eyebrows as he took in Elisha. "Damn, look at Matty go! No wonder you left us high and dry at that little honkytonk. Tucker didn't tell us the omega you were rushing off to save was such a pretty little thing."

"Easy, Luci. Don't make Matt kick your ass before we get a chance to say a proper hello." Nick was right beside him, playfully shoving Lucian aside. He walked up to Elisha and reached for his hand, bending over it to kiss the back and peering up at him with a flirtatious wink. "Howdy, honey. I'm Nick, and allow me to be the first to greet the only person who could have got this alpha of yours to come home."

Tucker and Devon made a point to also shove Lucian to the side so they could meet Elisha next. Reluctantly, I let go of his hand when Tucker held his arms out and asked for a hug. When Elisha hesitated, I leaned over to whisper in his ear. "Tucker is my best friend. He's safe. All of these guys are. They might joke around, but you can trust them."

Every one of them looked completely smitten when Elisha blushed. "I'm sorry. I'm hardwired to avoid alphas. I hope I didn't offend you." With that, he stepped into Tucker's outstretched arms.

I rested a hand on Elisha's back the whole time, so he knew I was there. "This is my buddy Tucker. He's probably my best friend in the whole world. Just don't let the other guys hear."

Lucian growled. "We're next to you, asshole. We have feelings too, you know."

"I've heard rumors along those lines." Grinning, I pulled Lucian into a hug. "It's damn good to see you, Luci. Thanks for riding out this way. I wasn't exaggerating when I said I need backup."

As I spoke, I checked on Elisha, talking quietly with Tucker and Devon. The bond told me he was calm and relaxed. For a second, I'd felt like a prick for dropping him in the deep end. When both of my worlds collided, it was easy to forget they were all meeting for the first time.

The hair on the back of my neck raised when Nick stiffened, as if going on alert. Glancing over my shoulder to see what had him alarmed, I immediately relaxed. Jared and the gammas were waiting on the porch. Nick was reacting to their palpable tension. I huffed and motioned for Jared to come over. As he quickly joined us, I focused my comments on Nick.

"Guys, I want you to meet the pack beta. If you'd like the historical dirt on me, Jared here is your best source. His father was the beta before him, so we grew up together. And yes, this bougey palace is my childhood home. Go ahead, let me have it."

Lucian whistled through his teeth and held the flaps of his WCW leather cut wide open to put his shirtless chest on full display. Most notably, the absence of the X-shaped scar over his heart. His big cheesy grin was a cover, silently daring Jared or any of the watching gammas not to notice he was a bastard.

"Check you out, Matt. Nobody's gonna want to hear my sad backstory when they're too busy feeling sorry for a poor little rich boy like you." To take any sting out of his teasing,

Lucian winked. "Seriously, though, nice digs. I bet walking away from a place like this was hard."

Nick leaned against Lucian, crossing his arms over his chest as he jerked his head back toward the gates. "What's up with your family living it up while the town fell to shit? I think I understand why you left."

Tucker cleared his throat. "Go easy on him, guys. Let's remember Matt arrived here two days ago. He was nice enough to give me the gate code, so obviously he's not gotten all above himself yet. How about we give him a chance to explain?"

Huffing a half-laugh, I held my palms up. "There is no excuse for this, Tucker. Nick was correct—the town is a shitty excuse of a living situation for my pack. Apparently, my uncle didn't give a shit. The least of the reasons I wish I'd killed him myself."

Devon, always the peacekeeper, smiled knowingly. "And I can imagine you've been kicking yourself for not checking on your pack a few years ago, am I right?"

Brushing a hand over my head, I let my breath out in a rush. "Among other things, Nicky. I had no idea my uncle challenged and killed my father after I left. He ran the pack into the ground, and don't get me started on how he treated Elisha. He deserved what he got. Which leads to why I called you guys here. Let me introduce you to my gammas real quick so we can go inside and start strategizing."

Nick clucked his tongue, shaking his head. "And here I was hoping you called us in for construction help. As soon as I laid eyes on your town, I figured rebuilding was at the top of your agenda."

"Oh, it definitely is, don't get it twisted. But first, I need to handle a few things. Starting with winning a challenge against Elisha's father."

Eyebrows raised all around. Lucian whistled again and glanced at Elisha. "You don't seem too upset. I take it your old man needs killing?"

I lifted my arm and slipped it around his shoulders when Elisha huddled against my side, blushing as he shrugged. "While I try not to advocate violence or wish death on people, my father did murder my bonded mate and leave me to die. If Matt hadn't shown up when he did and shown mercy by claiming me himself, the pack would be burying me right now." He spoke so candidly, his words became that much more heartbreaking.

Giving a firm nod, Lucian squared his shoulders. "Yep. Dude needs killing."

Turning, I led them toward the porch while I answered. "Yes, and I have to be the one to do it. You know pack law as well as the rest of us. In order to get my pack back and remove any claim he has on it, I have to challenge him. Avenging Elisha is just a bonus."

Elisha frowned at the thought of anyone dying on his behalf. I stopped to brush a kiss against his temple. "I said it was a bonus, little wolf. Not the reason I'm doing it. Remember I'll be saving the pack and your brothers in the process, if it'll help you sleep better."

Mentioning his little brothers was dirty pool, but Elisha immediately relaxed. After taking a moment to introduce my buddies to the gammas, we all headed back to the war room. The downstairs was as full as I'd seen it with nosy pack members trying to get a better look at the visiting alphas. After so many years away, I'd forgotten what an interesting occurrence this would be to them. A friendship like I shared with the West Coast Wolves was unheard of in our culture.

We chatted for about twenty minutes, breaking the ice

and explaining what we needed to so everyone was on the same page. Then Jared took a few minutes to go through some Council laws and teach me the official phrases I would need to make the challenge. By the time I was ready to contact the territory chief, the members of the two opposite groups were making small talk amongst themselves.

While their rapport was a good sign, the gammas were still unnerved. At least everyone seemed to be fine in the same room as I placed a call to the territory chief. Luckily, Jared had his cell number so I didn't have to go through his office. Putting it on speaker, I set the phone down in front of me so everyone could hear the conversation and leave no doubt what he had or had not said.

As the phone rang on the other end for the first time, the sound echoed around the room, making all of us cringe. I grimaced apologetically and left the volume where it was. Loud and obnoxious now, but necessary when the conversation began. After several rings, I was about to hang up when a deep, congenial-sounding voice rang out over the speaker.

"Hello there. This is TC Woodlawn. What can I do you for?"

"Good morning, TC Woodlawn. My name is Matt Longclaw. I'm calling on behalf of my home pack, Lucerne Valley."

TC Woodlawn sucked in an audible breath. "You're Bob's boy, I remember you. Forget the TC Woodlawn bullshit—call me Ash. If memory serves, I was stepping into my position around the time you left home. Caused quite a stir, let me tell you. And then your uncle showing up and taking the pack like he did was... well, it was something. Listen, son. I'm not sure what you think I can do for you, but I don't know if you want to challenge Monty Whitetail."

Turning to look into Elisha's eyes, I responded. "That is

exactly why I'm calling. I would like to request an official referee for a retaliatory alpha battle between myself and the alpha of Newberry Springs, Montgomery Whitetail. According to the rules given to us by the Supreme Wolf Council of the United States, I'm within my rights to issue a challenge. And not only do I have one valid reason, I have three."

"Aw, hell. This is why I hate Mondays. Go on then, tell me your three reasons." As soon as he finished speaking, he gulped and burped as china rattled in the background. Clearly, I'd interrupted his breakfast.

"You already know the first reason—this pack was my birthright. A Longclaw alpha has led Lucerne Valley since the pack was formed. Secondly, Alpha Whitetail challenged the previous alpha, my uncle, and won. His retaliatory challenge was based on my Uncle Horace stealing his omega son and claiming him for a mate. While this was true, Mr. Whitetail left out a few details when he presented his case to you."

TC Woodlawn tutted. "I don't know where you got your information, son. But I went over Monty's application with a fine-toothed comb. I know the man can be tricky, but his son Elisha was already promised to another pack's Alpha. I have a notarized statement from the deltas escorting him from Newberry Springs."

As much as hearing Elisha referred to merely as the omega rankled, I still smiled because I had the upper hand. "Correct, except for one small problem. Monty put the incorrect date on the application, and any notarized statements saying he was taken within the past ninety days are nothing but lies. The Lucerne Valley Gamma Council is ready to produce notarized statements stating Elisha has been part of this pack for the past six months."

"What a fucking liar. I thought for once he was telling the truth because there was proof. Let me guess, he waited six months because he was trying to work a deal with Horace?" TC Woodlawn's enraged tone went a long way toward making me respect the man. "And when Horace refused to pay up, Monty decided to use Council Law in his favor. Son of a bitch."

"If his lies aren't enough reason for me to issue a challenge, allow me to give you my third. Monty failed to provide an alpha to save his son after killing his bonded mate. When the pack reached out to me, Elisha was hours away from dying of aconite poisoning. I stepped up to save his life, first and foremost. In the process, I discovered Elisha is my true mate."

TC Woodlawn clucked his tongue against his teeth. "Damn straight it does. I'm guessing you don't want a first blood challenge—I believe you mentioned you wanted a retaliatory one?"

"Come on, Ash. You and I both know a ceremonial challenge would never work. I'd have to watch my back for the rest of my days. And chances are those wouldn't be long because Monty would find a way to get me in the back first chance he got."

"So you know what you will be dealing with, then. Okay, let me say unofficially I wish you the best. Now for the important part. Alpha Longclaw, as Territory Chief of the great state of California, I officially accept your reasons for placing a retaliatory challenge against Montgomery Whitetail of the Newberry Springs pack. The Alpha failed to provide a reasonable replacement for the First Mate of Lucerne Valley upon the death of his Alpha, and for this failure alone, the Supreme Wolf Council of the United States will support your right."

After a pause, his throaty chuckle burst into the room. "Official enough for you, Matt? Good talk, son. I'll be in touch with the time and date of your challenge. Until then, practice every dirty trick you've ever heard of because Monty will try them all."

"Thanks, Ash. Both for the heads up and your patience while I walked you through this whole sordid mess. I look forward to getting to know you better after this is all over. Maybe Lucerne Valley can finally put our fancy guest room to use, reserved for when you visit." After a little bit more small talk, the call ended, and I sat back to release a relieved breath.

Jared spoke first. "Do you think he meant it about Monty fighting dirty? Never mind, foolish question. Here's a better one—do you know how to fight dirty yourself?"

"If he doesn't, I know a few moves I've seen on the streets." Lucian spoke before I could answer. He glanced around the table with a knowing gaze. "I'd imagine we all know some sneaky tricks and bullshit moves we can help practice before he goes toe to toe with that fucker. No offense, Elisha."

Elisha quickly shook his head. "None taken. My father isn't a very nice man, and I've never met an alpha more deserving to lead this pack than Matt. My mate is too pure to fight dirty, so I'd appreciate all the help he can get to get ready. In fact, I can offer a few pointers because I've seen my father fight so many times, I can tell Matt which moves to anticipate."

While they all discussed how I should fight, I was thinking about what came after, when I would have two packs on my hands. If I won the challenge—*when* I won— they would both be rightfully mine. Considering the idea, I waited for a pause to discuss what Elisha brought up at breakfast. My mate was proving himself to be every bit as astute and forward-thinking as I'd expected. His observations and ideas were exactly what we needed around here. As soon as I saw my opening, I touched Elisha's hand to get his attention.

"Remember our earlier talk about the pack houses and how some members of the Newberry Springs pack might want to move here?" As he nodded, I continued. "I was thinking, and you're right. And along the same vein, some of our people might want to stay in their town. Although I do plan to put a stop to the criminal enterprises going on. But I keep coming back to this: at the end of the day, there will still be two separate packs. Even if they are all sworn to me, geography alone will keep us apart."

Elisha leaned back in his chair, resting his hands on his baby bump. "True. And it'll be difficult for us to focus on everything needing to be done here and do justice to the pack left over there. Do you have anything in mind, or did you want to talk it out?"

Smiling, I leaned in to kiss his cheek. "I love how logical you are, little wolf. And yes, I do have an idea, but I'd like your approval. Not simply because I want us to lead as a team, but Newberry Springs is your home pack, and none of us know them like you do."

"So what are you thinking?" His eyes lit with interest as he studied me.

"After I win the challenge, we've already agreed this town needs a lot of work. I'll be stretched too thin to go back and forth, especially with a baby on the way. What we need is another alpha. Someone willing to step up and run Newberry Springs with our blessing. Pack members can choose which one they want to stay with or move to, as the case may be. The ones here will help rebuild the town. The ones who go to Newberry Springs can help the new alpha decide the plan for whatever parts of the underground city aren't on government land."

Elisha slowly turned to look around the table. "Not only do I approve of your idea, but I think it's rather handy we have four alphas right here who you already trust."

Grinning from ear to ear, I turned to my friends. "I swear, it's like he can read my mind. Next question. Would any of you be interested in running the pack?"

Lucian was the lone one to shake his head no. "I'm not looking for a pack, you know that. No pack wanted me when I needed one, so I don't want one now. Bad blood aside, allow me to be the neutral party and ask what your intentions would be for whoever takes over Newberry Springs on your behalf. Are you looking at it as an offshoot of Lucerne Valley, and the alpha would answer to you? Or are you basically giving away a pack?"

Elisha grimaced leaning over the arm of the chair, so I met him halfway as he whispered in my ear. After he was finished, I had a better idea of how to answer. Elisha's thoughts were on the same page as my own, but his response was more concise and easy to explain.

"How I see it is we would understand our packs would always be connected as allies, but whatever alpha takes it over will take charge with my blessing. And since I will have won the pack and all its holdings by challenge, I'm within my rights to do this, and I don't need permission from anyone other than my mate, since Newberry Springs' property and holdings would be considered mine personally." I was pretty sure the Gamma Council knew as much, but it didn't hurt to clarify I wasn't giving away anything rightfully belonging to Lucerne Valley.

"Correct. If any pack members question it, I'll be happy

to show them the law pertaining to assets won in challenges." Jared frowned with concern, drumming his fingers on the arm of his chair. "My question is, are you sure you want to give it all away? The law states you could place a governing alpha in your stead. I don't know the value of their holdings, but I'd imagine you're leaving a lot of money behind."

I sat forward with my elbows on the table, looking around to make sure everyone was paying attention. "I'm absolutely certain I want to. Whoever takes over the second pack needs to have the freedom to do things their way. Some extenuating circumstances involving illegal mining have to be dealt with, and quite a few pack members won't be happy to see the money train go away. I won't ask anyone to put in the work it'll take over there and then tie their hands by making them come to me for permission about every decision."

Elisha spoke up in full agreement, making me proud. "Matt's right. Whoever takes over Newberry Springs needs the freedom to run it their way. As long as our packs remain allies, we will be happy to let it go. My heart lies here now, even before I met my true mate. I've never been happier than I've been in Lucerne Valley. I want to give our people the choice of which pack they want to be part of and then give each pack the chance to bloom separately while being allies."

"Well, damn. If I couldn't already tell the pair of you were made for each other, I'd know it now." Tucker smiled at me with suspiciously misty eyes. "For what it's worth, you can consider me as an option. As much as I love the West Coast Wolves, I don't know I have the heart to travel without you. And our goal has always been to help those in need, wouldn't you agree? Sounds to me like a pack out in that desert needs one of us. If anyone else is interested, choose whoever you think is best. I'm simply putting myself out there as an interested party."

Devon tilted his head toward Tucker. "What he said. All kidding aside, I'd be willing to step up for you, Matt. I don't care about what the assets might be worth, although I'm sure future me will be grateful if I'm chosen. But if you need me, I'm there."

When Nick hesitated, Lucian snorted. "If you're interested, now's the time to speak up. Listen, guys, Tucker was right about our moral code. I might want to kick my own ass one day for not jumping at the opportunity, but I'm not offended by you guys offering. Truth be told, maybe it's time we think about settling down. Putting down some roots. If two of us are going to be heading up packs, maybe the rest of us should consider getting a place nearby. Just because I don't want a pack of my own doesn't mean I wouldn't be down to visit you assholes when the mood strikes. I'm rambling, but I want you to know where my head's at."

We all laughed when Nick jumped up and ran around the table to give Lucian a big hug and a loud, smacking kiss on the cheek. Grunting, Luci tried to bat him away, but Nick held on like Velcro as he grinned at me. "Luci talked me into it, y'all. I'm tossing my hat in the ring too. Now Matt has to draw straws or come up with a good reason why he picked whoever he does, but there you go. Three alpha options, Matt. Have fun deciding."

I was still chuckling when my phone rang and picked it up without looking at the caller ID. Luckily, it was Ash. "Hey there, Matt. Letting you know the challenge is scheduled for one week from today at ten o'clock in the morning at a neutral spot in the desert between you. I'll text you the coordinates. Now this is where I'm supposed to suggest you get your affairs in order, should the challenge not go your way. But since my money's on you, I'll tell you to make sure you get a decent sleep the night before. Let's see, what else would a halfway decent parent tell you if they were here right now? I never had kids, so I wouldn't know. My mom would tell you to wear clean underwear and remember to brush your teeth, if her advice helps."

"Thanks, Ash. I'll take it under advisement. Or how about I let Elisha take charge and make sure I'm rested and well fed?"

Ash chuckled roughly in my ear. "Works for me too. Let your mate spoil the hell out of you, now that I think about it. Nothing will make you fight harder than knowing your sweet little mate is depending on you."

"Fuck you, Ash. Now I'm going to be stressing for the next week and remembering mine isn't the only life I'm risking." I held my breath, half afraid after talking to the territory chief like we were old friends.

I shouldn't have worried because Ash cracked up more. "Did you really say 'fuck you' to me? I like your style, kid. I knew I liked you. Now do us both a favor and don't screw this up. I'm looking forward to taking you up on your offer to visit your guestroom. In fact, I'll bring a bottle of my best scotch so we can toast your success."

"Sounds like a plan. See you Monday, Ash. I look forward to meeting you. I'll be the cocky one with four other alphas as my backup team. Yes, before you ask—there is a story. And I'll be happy to tell you all about it over a glass of scotch. Until then, I'll merely remind you Monty has all my deltas, and I have no other options."

Ash snorted. "Can't wait to hear the tale. A group of alphas working together? I wish I saw the like more often. Besides, you're welcome to bring anyone you want for your backup team. Hell, bring some damn cheerleaders and a marching band. Give us a show before the main event. Simply make sure you deliver at the end because I already know I'm going to prefer doing business with you."

"I'll do my best, Ash. Have the scotch ready."

EIGHT

ELISHA

Even though I had every faith Matt would win, tomorrow was scary to think about, so I was doing my best not to. Think about it, that was. And since I was having the best day ever, pretending we weren't one day away from the challenge was easy.

My life with Horace was nothing more than a bad dream at this point. After all the times I'd woken up to him pushing his fat, sweaty body into mine, waking up with my dick in my mate's mouth was amazing.

And afterwards, I'd been forced to take a long, hot shower where Matt took his time soaping me up and cleaning my body. He'd given special attention to every nook and cranny. Yeah... more than the temperature had been hot in our morning shower.

Paula was rattling around the kitchen when we went downstairs, but her presence was okay since I was supposed to be off today anyway. After shooing us to the breakfast room, Paula made sure we got to enjoy a private meal before letting anyone know where we were.

Sometimes, she could be too bossy, but days like this

reminded me how thankful I was to have her in my life. During my time with Horace, I'd wanted to take over managing the household because he wasn't as mean if he thought I was earning my keep. Plus, I really did enjoy cooking and meal planning. Housework, not so much. My role seemed to be changing anyway because I was mated to Matt, so it was probably a good thing Paula was so protective when it came to her job. Letting Paula work while I found other things needing my attention was easy.

Like my garden. Matt hadn't discovered my hideaway yet, and I'd been too shy to bring it up. But if he ever saw my lush plot, taking over the backyard with more fruits and vegetables than normal for the region, he might have a few questions.

And I wouldn't mind answering. I could trust Matt with anything... even my special secret. It was probably good I felt as much because my talent revealed itself sooner than I ever would've expected.

We were taking a walk through town with the gammas and Jared, until they'd split off to have a look at the well while Matt and I peeked at one of the residential areas. They wanted to go over the repair list we'd been putting together and decide which areas took top priority after getting the electricity restored. Matt's biker friends were here somewhere too, poking around and seeing if they could do anything to pitch in.

While I was thinking about all this, we were passing a small park when Matt stopped. "Hold on, little wolf. Why don't you stay back? I don't want you to trip over anything. The weeds are too overgrown to spot any hidden dangers. I want to find out if any of the playground equipment is salvageable, but I doubt it."

Shielding my eyes with my hand, I squinted at the rusty

metal structures. "I don't want to break your heart, but making anything on our playground kid-friendly will take a lot more than a coat of paint. I bet you'll find a complete overhaul is required when you check the structural integrity."

Matt hummed thoughtfully. "I'm right there with you. You can tell from here most of it is rusted clear through. Before I start ordering new equipment, I want to make sure I'm correct. I'm sure plenty would disagree, but I think it's important for the pack's pups to have a park. They need a safe place where they can run and let off some steam. Most of the houses have small yards, if you noticed."

My heart melted the same way it did every time Matt said something sweet and sensitive to the needs of others. I took a second look at the equipment but didn't have the heart to tell him he was wasting his time. I held back like he'd asked as he inspected everything from the play equipment to the worn-out benches and garbage containers.

While there wasn't anything I could do to help, a more important part of the park was right in my skill set: the grass and plants. I knelt and waved my hands over the weeds and dead husks, remnants of the small ornamental bushes lining the entryway once upon a time. Closing my eyes, I breathed in the burnt, sundried scent covering the natural smell of the dormant foliage.

Smiling as sunshine bathed my face, my eyes still closed, I felt around blindly for a shriveled blade of grass, hiding among the weeds. It took a few moments, but I discovered a good sample on the outside edge and pushed the force of my will toward the plant. Urging the few living cells remaining within the root pack to awaken and multiply, leaving a swath of new growth in their wake was easy as breathing.

Pinching either side of the blade with a gentle touch, I slowly stroked from bottom to top. It came to life between my fingers, smelling of fresh chlorophyll as the new plant cells winked awake. *Yes...* this would make the park green again. Especially if I worked slowly by sending fertilizer to town, charged and imbued with my special touch. Knowing I could give the children green grass to play on felt good. Hopefully by the time play equipment was installed, although doing too much at once might be risky.

Hmm... the bushes and flowers could come later. Since most people weren't gardeners, they probably wouldn't question how fast fertilizer could take effect. My eyes remained shut as I yanked a clump of dead crabgrass and sent a pulse of energy to all remaining plant cells, telling them it was okay to release and return to the cycle of nature. While I appreciated its hardy nature, we had no need for crabgrass in this park.

When I'd just finished sending a similar message to the weeds and dandelions, Matt's shocked voice nearly had me jumping out of my skin. "Elisha? What in the world happened here?"

My eyes flew open, and I winced at the sight of a two-by-two square inch area of bright, healthy green grass. And even worse, a green stripe had appeared on the previously assumed dead bush, where my arm brushed against it while I'd been focused on the grass. Matt squatted down in front of me to get a better look, his eyes glittering like a child meeting Santa.

Looking adorably confused, he met my eye. "Elisha, baby. I came over because I felt a wave of power through our bond. When I peeked over here, you looked like you were praying to the dead plants. And then I find this... I can't wrap my brain around it. What's going on?"

Tilting my head to the side, I listened carefully to make sure nobody was around. Matt shook his head. "Don't worry. We're completely alone. It's safe for you to talk."

I swallowed and smiled hopefully, throwing out jazz hands. "Umm... surprise? I can make magic happen."

Matt snorted so hard he started coughing. Knocking a fist against his chest, he shook his head with a rueful grin. "Not used to the desert dust again. Sorry. But also, keep in mind I already know your talent for magic. I sleep with you every night, remember?" I rolled my eyes when he wiggled his eyebrows.

"Not that kind of magic, silly. I mean, obviously. But shoot." I scratched my temple while I tried to figure out how to explain. Getting the words straight in my head, I puffed my cheeks out like a hamster and let out a gush of air before trying again.

"As you're aware, we omegas are pretty rare. What people don't know is why. My papa said the Supreme Council scratched it from our written history when the printing presses were invented and they could control the information getting out to the public. Papa claimed it was originally done to protect us. Then the practice continued to keep us omegas in our place. People who don't know our worth see us as freaky males who can give birth like a female."

"I've always wondered why such a rare kind of wolf was treated like a second-class citizen. It's never made sense to me. Even though I'm technically not your pup's sire, I love seeing your body ripe with new life. Knowing your gender doesn't make a difference in whether or not our family can grow is a miracle, in my book. But we're getting off track. I don't know how long we have before someone shows up, so I'm going to shut up and let you talk."

Laughing softly, I smiled at this wonderful man. My man. *Mine*. Gosh, would it ever get old to think about that?

Matt faked a cough. "I can feel your possessive affection through the bond. I love you too, little wolf. Now focus. Tell me why I'm looking at a green spot in a dead park."

"Sorry. So, yeah, whatever the reason, the end result is the same. Nobody knows the truth about omegas. I'm going to give you the bare-bones version, since we're short on time. Basically, an omega can only be born through one of two ways. Either a true mate pairing between two shifters, no matter the status of the parents. The other way is from an alpha and omega match—like my parents."

"Explains why there are so few of you. Not many of us are lucky enough to find our true mate, and without a lot of omegas available, the number of alpha and omega pairings are limited too."

Nodding, I continued. "Yes, exactly right. And since childbirth is harder on our bodies, omegas don't usually have as many children as our female counterparts. Multiples are super rare. Thankfully so because our hips aren't made to carry twins or triplets as easily as a female's."

When I started to look around and listen again, Matt was quick to reassure me. "Don't worry, Elisha. My wolf is on alert. We'll know if anyone approaches long before they can overhear anything you have to say."

Taking a deep breath, I forced myself to tell him the freaky part. "So what nobody knows is every omega has their own special gift or talent. We don't dare let anyone in on our secret when we're already at risk of being stolen like I was. Except for true mates, who can sense it through the bond like you did. Or people we can trust. It doesn't show up until the stage between childhood and puberty. Papa was watching closely for signs of my gift so he could teach me to hide it without my father ever finding out, and I did the same with my brother Saul last year."

Matt closed his eyes as he slowly nodded in understanding. "Yet another reason why we need to save your brothers." Opening his eyes, he motioned toward the greenery. "So your gift is bringing dead plants back to life?"

Giggling, I shook my head and held my thumb up. "I prefer to think of it as having the ultimate green thumb. In fact, I was musing earlier how I should show you my garden. Paula believes I have special plant food and fertilizers. There aren't many gardeners in this pack, and the ones here think you drop the seed into the ground, water it, and pull a few weeds while you wait for Mother Nature to decide what you get."

"Good for you, though. It definitely works in your favor. You'll have to show me your garden when we get home—I'm intrigued. It also explains how we had kiwi in the fruit salad yesterday. You could've ordered it, but the produce normally shipped this way isn't as fresh and juicy as the meals you've been serving me."

"Thank you for noticing. It makes me happy." Hello, understatement of the year. From the look on his face, Matt could feel my joy through the bond. In my defense, having my efforts appreciated really was nice. "Oh! And wait till you see the flower garden. All the fresh flowers around our home come from there."

Matt leaned forward for a kiss, his lips brushing softly over mine and sending goosebumps down my arms. We smiled at each other as he pulled back, contentment flowing through our bond. "I always notice you, Elisha. And everything you do. From what I've seen so far, you're nothing short of amazing. And I thought so before I saw your ultimate green thumb magic. Is there a restriction to what you can do? And is it okay to ask what other kinds of gifts omegas are blessed with?"

"So far I haven't found my limits, but then, I've always had to be careful, so I haven't had a lot of time or privacy to try. As for other omega gifts, they can include anything involving the natural world from psychic powers, to being able to heal anything short of death with a touch, to controlling the weather. And even though you know, don't ever ask an omega about their gift unless they offer to tell you or you accidentally catch them at it. It's truly the sole thing many omegas have to protect themselves."

"Speaking of, as much as I love seeing the proof of your abilities, I think it's probably best if we hide it, yeah?" As soon as I nodded, Matt was on his feet. He looked around and said "gotcha" when he spotted one of the trash cans—or wooden barrels, in this case—left here to rot. Surprisingly, the thing still seemed strong as he carried it over. I carefully pushed up and stepped out of the way while Matt placed it precisely over the small patch of grass and shoved it up against the stripe in the bush. Wiping his hands on his hips, he stepped back with a look of satisfaction.

"This should do it, don't you think? If anyone moves the barrel, they'll think trapped moisture worked wonders or something. Right?" He stopped and rubbed the back of his neck, looking at the barrel and second-guessing himself. "The logic doesn't work, though, because plants need sunshine to grow."

Laughing, I hooked my arm through his and tugged him toward the sidewalk. "It's perfect, my love. And you're perfect for thinking of it. Believe me, people are more willing to take things at face value than you'd think. If anybody happened to move the barrel in the next few minutes, they'd shrug and say 'cool' before getting on with their life. Covering it gave anyone who might come along later the perfect reason not to overthink it."

"Good point. I would've reacted the same way. Now I don't know about you, but I'm ready to track everyone down and head home. We have the big potluck tonight, and I'd kind of like to take a nap before I have to give my rah-rah speech so our people don't worry when I step into the challenge ring tomorrow morning. I want them to see me confident to the point of looking cocky."

Imagining all we had left to do today made me want to nap along with him. Paula hadn't allowed me to be involved with the planning or any preparations for our first party with our new Alpha tonight. She told me my job was to relax and enjoy being newly mated. But I would still be making the rounds during the party, ensuring everyone was getting enough to eat and having a good time. Matt was correct—we needed to keep morale high. If for no other reason than so Matt wouldn't be distracted during the challenge tomorrow.

"Are you planning to announce which alpha you have chosen to take over Newberry Springs during your speech?" I thought I knew the answer before asking the question, but I was nosy enough to pry. Especially when my mate had been tightlipped about the whole thing while considering the decision.

"Yes. I've decided to give Newberry Springs to Nick. He's the smartest guy I know and well-versed in both shifter and human laws. Given the amount of criminal activity your father has going on, someone like him is needed to sort through it all and make things square. Devon is too much of a peacekeeper, and the miners who don't want to stop digging for gold will walk right over him. As for Tucker, he would also be a good choice, but I have two problems picking him. One, it almost feels like I'm playing favorites if I chose my best friend. And two, and this is the biggest reason, Tucker is claustrophobic as hell. I can't see him going near an underground tunnel, let alone dealing with an entire underground town."

"I don't think you need to worry about your closeness with him. The claustrophobia part, though, would be a problem. Making sure the miners aren't still breaking laws and mining on government property is impossible if he can't go see for himself. Scenting lies only works with people who feel guilty. If a shifter is hardened enough, they can lie to your face without anyone picking up a thing. I know this because I've seen it more than once among my father's cronies. Nick doesn't have an easy job ahead of him, take it from me." I fell silent for a few steps before glancing back at Matt. "It's a shame Lucian feels unworthy because he doesn't carry a sire scar. He shouldn't let the circumstances of his birth define his future."

Matt released a deep sigh. "You're not saying anything I don't feel, little wolf. We've been telling Lucian for years how he has more to offer than he thinks. He might be a flirtatious manwhore, but the guy has a heart of gold. And he's beyond talented in so many ways. Someday he's going to fall in love and find the sense of home he was denied growing up. Maybe then he'll be able to let go of the past and start seeing the man the rest of us do. In the meantime, the people who love him will keep encouraging him to be his best self."

Our conversation came to a halt because Lucian himself approached from the opposite direction with Nick at his side. Matt shocked a giggle out of me, scooping me up and double-timing it to catch up with his friends. As I relaxed into the powerful arms holding me so close, I said a quiet prayer for tomorrow... and all the tomorrows hinging on his success.

And then I said another prayer for forgiveness when I realized I was literally praying for my father's death. But he'd left me to die, and besides, the safety of my brothers and every member of both packs depended on Matt winning. I doubled down, praying twice as hard for Matt's success. I even reached out for my secret weapon... the one person I knew who might have an 'in' with the big man upstairs.

If you're listening, Papa, please put a good word in for Matt. You know better than anyone: he's the best option all the way around. I'm prejudiced because he's my true mate, but if you've been watching, then you already know my mate is a good alpha. Watch over him for me tomorrow, if you can.

NINE

MATT

Any nerves I had over the past week building up to the moment were gone. I was riding in the lead position with my buddies directly behind me in pairs.

As for the convoy of ragtag vehicles following us... I was doing my best not to think about them. I'd tried to convince Elisha to wait at home, but he was determined to be here today. When he shared his plans with me over breakfast this morning, my wolf and I both wanted to deny his request.

I had no doubt about my ability to win any fair fight, but I wasn't cocky enough to think I couldn't be bested by an alpha known for fighting dirty. While I wasn't enthused about killing his father in front of him, I couldn't deny Elisha the right to bear witness.

I still wanted to fight him on it until Tucker took me aside, after he'd walked into the kitchen and felt the tension in the room. Once Tucker gently reminded me how devastated Elisha would be if the worst happened, it took no more than a few seconds for me to agree.

Not merely his reminder, but I'd made my own backup plan with Tucker. While they wouldn't share a true mate bond, if Monty beat me, Tucker would jump in and immediately challenge Monty on the spot in order to save Elisha from the same fate he'd faced nine short days ago. And the pup as well.

With Elisha standing there visibly pregnant, Ash would have no reason to refuse a challenge to save him. And even better, Monty would be worn out from the fight and easier to kill. My backup plan hadn't thrilled Elisha, but he'd given me his word to choose life and allow Tucker to claim him.

I might've used the pup to plead my case, but he'd only agreed because he had every faith I would walk away the winner today. And I shared his certainty. Mostly. As my grandma liked to say, the only certain things in life were death and taxes. So while I was betting on me, I wasn't ignoring the other possible outcome.

But right here and now, with the sunshine on my face, the wind at my back, and the powerful Harley engine between my legs—I was liking my chances. I might have had ninety-nine problems, but fear wasn't one. Letting go of the handlebars, I held my arms straight out and let my wolf come forward enough to howl, riding between two rows of delta wolves at parade stance.

As we drew close to the large crowd of people waiting around the fighting ring, the other guys receded. I gripped my handlebars again and revved my engine before swerving to a stop, bringing my bike sideways with a flurry of pure desert dust. Alpha Whitetail caught a face full, which was a pleasant bonus.

I was off the bike with my helmet and gloves removed before Monty could make his way over. I was never letting him have the upper hand, even if it was merely perception. As he stalked toward me with an ugly look on his face like he smelled something bad, I sized him up, standing my ground.

I'd seen him in passing when I was a kid, and my memory hadn't been wrong. A head shorter than me and with far less bulk, he was one of those scrawny types who made up for physical lacking with pure meanness. Still, I wouldn't count him out. While on the smaller side, he gave the impression of sinewy muscles and tightly coiled strength. He might not have been the biggest alpha on the block, but he would strike like a cobra if given a chance.

I'd gone shirtless under my leather cut, putting my tattooed arms and bulging biceps on display when I crossed my arms over my chest. My WCW members walked up behind me, but I kept my attention focused on Monty. Despite the crowd of witnesses, I knew better than to look away. A shiv to the gut would save time in the ring. At least, most men like him would think so.

He walked so close we were nearly toe to toe, looking up at me with the ease of a lifetime of being a shorter alpha. "So you're Bob Longclaw's kid, huh? You look different than I remember. But I guess you would, wouldn't you? Probably don't like folks remembering you as the scared, sniveling pup hiding in his daddy's shadow. At least your uncle had the balls to look your father in the eye when he challenged him for the pack."

"Horace didn't have to concern himself with saving the Alpha Mate's life. He saw a pack he wanted and took it. I chose to save a life and accept the pack along with it. As for looking you in the eye, I'm here now, and I'm definitely looking. Not for nothing, but you seem like the kind of narcissistic prick who would leave his own son to die after killing his mate."

Monty spat a foul wad of tobacco on the ground.

"Sucker deserved killing. Thieving bastard took my property. If the fool kid didn't know how to escape, he's obviously no son of mine. I thought I'd washed my hands of him, so imagine my surprise feeling a loss in the pack bond. Sure, it wasn't more than a chunk of weaker pack members left to hold down the fort in Lucerne, but they wasn't yours to take. Neither was my kid. He shoulda faced his fate like a man."

I knew Elisha was approaching, but Monty hadn't been paying attention to anyone but me. At Elisha's sharp gasp, he jerked. Anger coiled in my gut at the hurt etched on my sweet little wolf's face. When Monty started talking again, it was all I could do to clench my fists and remember these were the words of a dying man. Monty was going down.

"Speak of the devil and here comes my runt. Stand up straight, boy. Don't embarrass me any more than you already are by being here." Monty glared back at me. "What kind of an alpha doesn't know to leave the omega at home? Especially one so fat with a dead man's pup. I don't know what to make of you, son. But if you're gonna let your omega boss you around, maybe I'll be doing you a service helping you find your way out of this world today."

My teeth were clenched so tightly I could barely speak properly. "I'm not your son, thank fuck. As for the single person present who actually is? Elisha is my equal, not my property or a thing to be hidden. You don't get to talk to him. Hell, I don't want you even looking at him. He might be my equal, but Elisha is also mine to protect. And avenge. If you think I'm challenging you because of Horace or the pack you stole, think again. Reclaiming the Lucerne Valley pack members is secondary to repaying you for nearly causing Elisha's death."

Monty's answering smile didn't reach his cold, flat eyes. "Mighty brave words from a dying man. Maybe someone will carve your lofty bullshit on your tombstone. Yeah, the part about you thinking an omega could ever be equal to an alpha will look mighty poetic until your grave marker fades and crumbles under the desert sun, like the bones of you and that omega you're so hell-bent on protecting."

When I growled, a man somewhere between us in height rushed up and pushed us apart. I prepared to tell the stocky, dark-haired man with gray at the temples to fuck off. So fast it nearly knocked me on my ass, a powerful wave of alpha pheromones came off him. I didn't need the badge pinned to his chest to know who'd interrupted us.

I gave a terse nod. "TC Woodlawn, I presume. It's a pleasure to meet you, sir."

After Monty and I both took a full step back, he dropped his hands with an *aw, shucks* grin. "Come on now. I already told you to call me Ash. How about we forget this business here and take it into the ring where it belongs?" Turning, he waved a hand toward the large, circular area raked free of loose rocks or plants and bordered with a ring of evenly sized stones. Even now, the spectators took their places around the circle, placing bets and getting ready for the spectacle of violence they had come to see.

Ash turned back, lifting an eyebrow as if asking for my approval. "As guaranteed by Supreme Council rule, you've got one brand-new, unused, regulation-sized challenge ring ready to go. You're welcome to measure it, of course. I can promise my own personal deltas built it, and we've had eyes on it since it was completed to prevent any tampering."

My nostrils flared as I sucked in a deep breath. Jerking my head from side to side to stretch my neck, I huffed my approval. "Looks good enough to me, Ash. And even if it didn't, I would still respect you enough to take you at your word. Anything I need to know before we proceed?"

Glancing back and forth between Monty and me, Ash ran over the basic rules. "Y'all already know what's what, but I have to tell you anyway. Since both of you have already agreed this is to be a full challenge and not a first blood duel, those rules apply. You can take as long as you want to step inside the ring, but once you do, nobody leaves until we have a clear winner. Two will enter, and one will leave. You will fight as wolves. No human weapons are allowed. If you shift and illegally win the challenge with a weapon, you will be disqualified, and both packs will go to the fallen alpha. The Gamma Council of the winning pack will choose a new alpha in the fallen one's place. Any questions?"

Monty grunted. "Only one. Are we done with all the chin-wagging? Because I've got work waiting for me when I get done with this bullshit." I snorted at his arrogance but let it go.

Nodding to Ash, I turned and held my arms out for the mate I already heard coming. Elisha grabbed my shoulders, hugging me tight while he whispered a final warning. "I remembered something. Keep an eye on my father's ears. When he feints right or left, the opposite one will twitch. Ignore the rest of his body language and prepare to be struck from whichever side gives a twitch."

I chuckled softly as I kissed his neck. "Most mates would be begging me to rethink this or swearing their undying love. It says a lot about you how your last words to me before the fight are to offer advice."

"Because I'm strong in my trust, and I know you're going to win. I'll accept no other outcome. Don't drag it out, though. It's getting hot."

"God, I love you." My hands slid down his back to give his ass a squeeze. "Thank you for this, Elisha. Your faith is everything to me."

We shared a fast, passionate kiss before he patted my cheek. "I love you too. Now get in there and do me proud, *son.*" When he repeated 'son' in the same condescending tone his father used, I snorted. I couldn't wait to get this over with and spend the rest of my life loving my fascinating man.

I made quick work of undressing, passing my boots, jeans, and my WCW cut into Elisha's care. Jared stood beside Elisha, while my gamma wolves surprised me by shifting in solidarity. Tucker and the rest of my crew had also shifted, waiting to follow me to the ring.

The two parade lines of deltas had already shifted, pushing themselves between the right side of the ring and the crowd. While they might not all have truly supported Monty, they were forced to be his backup. Altogether, at least three, if not four, dozen of them clustered together, growling a lupine version of smack talk.

I could never unsee Monty's scrawny ass and surprisingly hairy back, and watching him shift into a mangy gray and white wolf was a relief. He snarled over his shoulder before stepping into the ring. Unwilling to be intimidated, I tapped the left side of my mouth to let him know I'd noticed the broken, yellow fang he was sporting. I laughed and flipped him off when he snarled again. Only then did I let myself shift.

Calling my wolf forward, I gave into his thrall and let him take control. My bones cracked and popped, reforming and changing in an instant. Gums burning, my jaw stretched, and the teeth elongated. Closing my eyes, I enjoyed the tingling rush as fur replaced skin. When my hands curled into claws, I fell forward onto four strong paws. I opened my eyes and took in the scene with newly enhanced vision.

In human form, I enjoyed better stronger senses than the average person—but there was nothing like being in furskin. I smelled each and every person present, no matter what form. Along with their ordinary scents was a heady mix of fear, loathing, and deceit from Monty and his cronies. Pride, love, hope, and faith came from those rooting for me. A lot of the hope came from the deltas backing Monty, and I was glad all over again about doing the right thing when Jared called.

While Elisha would always be my first priority, knowing two packs needed my help made me proud to give it. Before I stepped a paw toward the ring, I looked back over my shoulder for a final glance at the person who mattered more than anything in the world. When I wagged my tail, Elisha grinned and rolled his eyes, motioning for me to get going.

I chuffed a wolfie laugh and sprang forward, loving my strong muscles as I bounded into the ring and ran in a circle around Monty. Stopping in front of him, I braced myself on all fours and greeted him with a drooling snarl.

Sounding almost joyful, Ash shouted from the side. "Hell yeah. Let the games begin."

Though my eight-wolf backup committee encouraged me from outside the ring, I kept my attention completely focused on Monty. I blocked out the snarls and growls from his cheering section, lowering my chest to the earth and playfully wagging my tail. As I expected, he underestimated my youth and bought the puppy act. His jaw was wide open and ready to close around my neck as he jumped forward. Rolling quickly to the right, I was back on my feet with his white tail gripped between my teeth before he saw me coming.

Catching another alpha by the tail was a low, undignified blow. Since Elisha told me it was one of his signature moves, I bit down and pulverized the top joints between my back teeth. His indignant, pain-filled yelp pleased my wolf. As Monty jerked around sideways to come for my throat again, I snapped my head to the right and released his tail, sending him sliding a few feet away. He would've gone farther, but Monty was a scrappy fighter.

Scrambling at the ground, he found traction by digging his claws into the sand. He came running right back at me, feinting right and coming in low, aiming for a belly bite. I barely had a split second to react. Thanks to Elisha's last-minute advice, I knew to move right when his left ear twitched. Our fight went on with him attacking and me knowing which direction to dodge for what felt like an hour but was probably mere minutes. He might have been older and out of shape, but Monty's dirty fighting made the challenge last longer than necessary.

Panting heavily now, Monty tried to sneak up from behind when I was mid-roll after evading another belly attack. When he struck, I kicked his chest with my back feet and flipped him over. In a heartbeat, I locked my jaw around the softest part of his throat.

My wolf didn't hesitate the way I might've. Our laniary fangs were already in position, carrying the Medeina venom. Once I delivered the kill bite, I let him go and stepped back to watch him die. Immediately paralyzed, Monty didn't go out with a whine or a yelp. As the poison spread through his blood stream, he looked me directly in the eye, snarling and growling the whole time. At the end, his body became a confusing mess of skin and fur, shifting back and forth between forms, unable to hold either one.

When his heart beat its last, I was glad he was back in wolf form because it was easier for Elisha. Through our bond came a hint of sorrow at his sire's passing, but nothing more than a hint. His prevailing emotions were pride, joy, and relief.

Shifting, I held my arms out and stepped forward to meet Elisha, running into the ring to fling his arms around me again. His face was wet with tears I quickly kissed away. Shuddering, he submitted to my touch, smiling sweetly as I brushed the back of my fingers across his cheek. "Don't cry, little wolf. This was the only good outcome today, remember?"

Elisha quickly shook his head. As he planted his hands on my chest, his eyes radiated the relief pulsing through our bond. "No, Matt. I'm crying because it's stupid pregnancy hormones. And because I'm happy. I knew you could do it, and you did. Now we can find my brothers and get on with living our lives. And if anyone thinks I'm callous for not crying over my father's death, they can kiss my ass."

"No they can't. Nobody gets to kiss that sweet ass but me." Winking, I touched my forehead against his and breathed in his scent. I didn't raise my head until Ash reached our sides.

After respectfully nodding to Elisha, Ash turned and clapped me on the shoulder. "Congratulations, Matt. Allow me to officially be the first to say Montgomery Whitetail is dead. I hereby declare in front of all these witnesses: you, Matthias Longclaw, have won the challenge. The Newberry Springs pack and all its holdings are now yours to do with as you will. Obviously, the aforementioned holdings include any pack-owned property, the pack itself, and any personal items or wealth belonging to the deceased. This is fair, accepted by the Supreme Wolf Council and understood by the Newberry Springs pack before the challenge was accepted."

I looked around at the crowd and the few men trembling in their wolf forms. Most of the deltas had shifted back, but those closest to Monty were clearly waiting for me to behave as he would've if the situation had been reversed. With Elisha at my side, I walked to the center of the ring and tried to deliver what I hoped would be a short but succinct speech.

"Good morning. For those of you who will mourn his passing, allow me to offer my condolences for your loss. Understand, I offer this out of kindness because I entered this challenge intending the outcome lying in front of us. And my reason has everything to do with the man standing beside me. Newberry Springs Pack, you know Elisha as one of your own. He didn't ask for the hand fate dealt him when he was stolen by one alpha and left to die six months later by another. I'm only here today because I answered a call from the concerned beta at Lucerne Valley, begging me to save Elisha's life. Everything I've won today is secondary to my mate."

The chorus of shocked murmurs spreading through the pack told the truth. Monty hadn't mentioned Elisha's fate. I let the knowledge settle in before continuing. "Those of you who came to Newberry Springs from Lucerne Valley might recognize me as the alpha heir who walked away ten years ago, rather than accept the leadership of my own father when I came of age. I left because, like Elisha's, my father was abusive and hardly the kind of Alpha I wanted to serve. I'm not like him, and Lucerne Valley will be run differently under my control, which leads me to my next point of business. I have neither the time nor energy to run two packs, especially with a pup on the way." I waited for the chuckles and soft awws to die down before I got to the meat of it.

"Here's the most important point of business I have with

you today. As you heard our territory chief say, Newberry Springs is mine to do with as I please. I have decided our packs will remain allies, but I'm giving control of Newberry Springs and its holdings to my friend, Nick Jackson. Nick is a good man and an even stronger alpha. I would trust no one else more to have my back in a fight. As a second-born alpha son, he was forced out of his pack and left to be a lone wolf because of our ridiculous customs. His home pack's loss will be your gain."

Turning my head, I motioned for Nick to join me. He stood at my left side with a confident air. I bumped my shoulder against his, then turned back to the crowd. "At this time, I would like everyone who wishes to remain with the Newberry Springs pack to move to Nick's side of the circle. If you wish to return to Lucerne Valley, or move there for the first time and leave Newberry Springs behind you, please stand over here, on my side. And now, I'll give Nick a chance to talk because I've jabbered long enough."

Chuckling, Nick returned my shoulder bump from before. "Thanks, Matt. I want to second everything Matt just told you. There will be no hard feelings if any of you choose Lucerne Valley over Newberry Springs. There will also be no repercussions for anyone who backed your former Alpha today, even if it was at your own choosing. Some major changes will be happening in Newberry Springs. Elisha was kind enough to bring me up to speed on all your operations, but we will deal with that later. After I have a chance to meet with your current Gamma Council when I get over there, I will decide which ones, if any, will remain in a leadership role. Any of you deltas who want to be promoted to gamma level might have an opportunity."

Pausing, Nick glanced at Ash. "Elisha has also informed me Newberry Springs doesn't currently have an epsilon in residence, unless things have changed in the past six months? If not, I would like to catch you after we're done to officially announce the opening and request for one to visit until the position can be permanently filled. If I'm going to transfer gamma powers from the outgoing members to any worthy deltas, I'll need an epsilon to make it happen."

"Sure thing, and I'll be happy to help out. It'll be a pleasure working with you. I can feel it in my bones." Ash radiated pride and contentment, making it obvious he supported my decision.

Nick clapped his hands, then rubbed his palms together. "All right. Pick your poison—I mean, your pack." The sense of intrigued relief from the Newberry Springs people was palpable. "And so you know, when we get over to town, I'll be making this same offer to any pack members who aren't present to choose for themselves."

Speeches finished, Nick and I shook hands, and he promised all new and returning Lucerne Valley pack members would arrive by sunset the following day. As I hugged him, I couldn't help but think how weird riding back to pack lands without Nick would feel. Even though I knew this was a good decision all around, change was hard. Especially after we'd ridden together for so long.

Touching his forehead to mine, Nick clasped my neck and settled my frayed nerves. "We all hate change, Matty boy. But you said it yourself: our packs will be allies, and I'll always be a phone call and a ride away. Thank you for the gift you're giving me. This is going to be fun."

I pulled away, laughing and shaking my head. "Only you would walk into the situation Elisha prepared you for and call it fun."

Nick winked. "You forget, citing the law is fun for me.

Fun, fun, fun. Maybe if we say it enough times, you'll believe it."

We reluctantly let each other go to greet our new pack members. Remembering Elisha's request, I kept it short and simple. "Thanks for choosing Lucerne Valley. Let's save our official introductions and swearing allegiance to me as your Alpha until we get back over there. It's damned hot out here, and a reception with plenty of ice cold beverages waits for us back at our pack lands."

With that, I escorted Elisha to his car, leaving Monty's body for Ash to dispose of however he saw fit. Squeezing Elisha's hand, I spoke barely loud enough for him to hear. "Let's go home, little wolf."

TEN

ELISHA

After Paula's fabulous luncheon, I really wanted a nap. But since anyone with a brain knew there's no rest for the weary, I got to work instead.

While Matt was biting wrists, greeting pups, and sizing up his deltas, Jared and I got busy assigning homes for the new pack members who had sworn their allegiance. The rest of their families wouldn't be here until tomorrow, but we were determined they would have homes waiting for them.

The unmated deltas were the easiest because we had the upstairs dorms for them, since the rest of the pack would be moving back to their own homes. Matt and I had already agreed incoming members could have a ninety-day settling-in period before they decided whether to rent or buy the pack housing we had to offer.

I was going down the list under my breath, making notes of everything necessary, when someone cleared their throat. Glancing up, I was prepared to answer their question and quickly send them on their way, but I found myself smiling instead at a familiar face.

"Christina! I never thought I'd see you again—when did you get here?" I searched the room for the rest of her family, waving at her mate and their children and gasping with delight when I saw her elderly parents seated with them. Setting my clipboard aside, I hugged my former teacher and allowed myself a few moments of break time.

After rocking me from side to side, Christina held me at arm's length with a firm grip on both of my hands. "Let me get a look at you, Eli. Gracious, your papa would be so proud of you right now. And hubba hubba, by the way. Congrats on the hot alpha. Does this mean I have to be official now and call you Alpha Mate?" Even though she'd been one of my tutors, Christina was hardly ten years older than me, and we'd been good friends when I was younger.

"God, no." I dramatically shuddered at the very idea. "I have already told everyone here to call me Elisha. I don't need any fancy titles. Or, in your case, Eli." Smiling, I squeezed her hands. "I'm so happy to see you. I was hoping your family would choose to change packs, but I wasn't sure how Tony would feel about it. How are you here so soon? We aren't expecting the Newberry Springs people until tomorrow, except for the deltas who wanted to come swear allegiance today."

Releasing my hands, Christina waved dismissively. "Oh, honey. We were so done with that pack. Tony called as soon as he could and told me to meet him here. In fact, Tony only went today because he planned to ask the territory chief about transferring. Everything we own was already packed and loaded. My parents, too. As much as I wanted to stick around and try to keep an eye on your brothers, I couldn't risk staying much longer. My sons were never going to become miners, especially with some illegal scheme like

Alpha Monty had going on. We had to be careful and wait for the perfect time to escape."

"Looks like you found it." I hesitated before asking the important question. "My brothers... are they okay?"

Her face softened into a loving smile. "Don't worry—they've been fine. The pack has been keeping a close watch on both of them in your absence. I'm so sorry you went through everything you did, even if it worked out in the end. Nobody should be traded like chattel in the first place. The Supreme Council needs to do better by you omegas. They're able to keep your poor treatment swept under the rug because of the steps every pack has to hide pregnant omegas from any watching humans. Their judgment shouldn't matter. Maybe one day, we'll get the right leadership, and they'll do away with it."

"You're preaching to the choir, Christina. But omegas will remain second-class citizens in our society until we get Supreme Council members who have a true mate or omega child. Things won't change until the people in power have a personal reason to make it happen. We make up such a small segment of our society, so most wolves easily pretend our mistreatment and abuse isn't happening." I took a deep breath, blowing my frustrations away as I expelled it. "Enough about the Supreme Council. I have too much on my plate to worry about things I can't change today. It's a good thing you have all your things with you because we're headed to town after this to assign housing."

Christina grimaced, reeking of embarrassment. "Can I be frank?"

Wrinkling my nose, I shrugged one shoulder. "I mean, you could try? But I like you as Christina. Frank is a grouchy old thing with serious halitosis issues." He really was too. Mostly because he preferred to go hunting in wolf form and eat his prey fresh. To each his own, but would it kill the man to brush his teeth when he got back home? Especially before mingling with pack members.

"If I were still your teacher, I would make you write sentences for such an awful joke." She rolled her eyes, then returned to her point. "I wasn't too impressed by what we saw when we came through town. Are all the houses quite so... dilapidated?"

"Unfortunately, yes. The worst of them have been tagged for repairs before anyone can move in. But we have a good number of empty homes to offer nevertheless." I explained the plan for handling the houses. "And even better? The Gamma Council has already approved pack monies for the most necessary repairs required to make the houses habitable. You'll have to pay for fresh paint and new carpets, but the important things will be purchased by the pack."

As she nodded thoughtfully, her eyes glittered with interest. "How very democratic of you guys. I like that. Now it's merely a question of whether or not Tony and I can tackle the harder things when we start fixing our place up because I'm sure there will be a lot, after what I saw."

Jared walked up in time to hear her thoughts. After introducing himself, he grinned from ear to ear, delivering news I hadn't known yet. "Thanks to a few of the Newberry Springs deltas who apparently used to work for the power company, I can at least promise electricity. Something I couldn't have offered an hour ago. Our town has been without it for longer than I care to admit."

My eyebrows shot up. "Seriously? They were able to fix it so easily?"

"Seriously. I drove down the hill to see it for myself. Store lights are on all up and down Main Street, and I saw more than one porch light left on when the power blew. It's amazing what can be done when people around you know how to handle those kinds of things."

Jared and I shared a relieved smile. The power situation had been stressing us both out. Asking our own pack, let alone ones who chose to take Matt up on his offer, to move to a place where even the most basic of utilities wasn't available was unfair. As a new idea occurred to me, I bounced. "While we're assigning housing today, we should take note of special skills. What if people could trade their expertise, and everyone could work together to help fix all the houses? And everything else this town needs?"

His eyes lit as he nodded, already seeming to have been thinking along the same lines. "Obviously, the pack will pay people for their work on municipal projects, but I was going to suggest working together and bartering skills to get the residential repairs accomplished. But trading back and forth to beautify their homes and handle the upkeep we aren't responsible for providing would benefit everyone."

Christina squealed softly with delight. "I was already excited about moving here. Now I'm ecstatic. One more question, and then I'm going to let you get back to work. Are all the homes the same size, or do you have any big enough to enable my parents to live with us? With them getting up there in years, I worry about them living alone. Dad has mobility issues, and Mom's memory isn't what it used to be."

I picked up my clipboard and pointed to a property suiting her needs. "Not only do we have different-sized homes to offer depending on family size, there are several with in-law suites. I think you'd like this one here best. It has four bedrooms, so all three of your pups would have their own room, and there's an apartment with a separate entrance, so your parents could live there without things feeling crowded for either of you. And even better, it's across the street from the community park we're planning to reopen soon."

My clipboard smashed against my chest when Christina spontaneously hugged me. As she squealed in my ear, I tried not to wince. "Thank you, Eli. Thank you, thank you, thank you. This home sounds perfect and way better than anything I could've hoped for. Quick, put my name down before anyone else finds out about it."

After another hug, she left to tell Tony the exciting news, while I assigned the first house of the day, sight unseen. The rest of the afternoon was a blur of showing houses to the people we thought they would suit and making the official assignments. At each home, Jared gave them their key and a small plant I'd provided as a welcome gift. If everybody assumed the plants had come from an order I'd made through a local nursery, the idea was fine with me. Putting my gift to use just felt good.

Matt and I ended the day in our suite, sitting on our small loveseat while a program played on the TV. I was lying back against the opposite arm with my feet in Matt's lap after he insisted on massaging them.

Sniffing in satisfaction, Matt smiled at the fragrance of the peppermint lotion he was rubbing in. I giggled and kicked involuntarily when he hit a ticklish spot. Fortunately, his reflexes kept him from taking it in the chin. I shrank my head down into my shoulders. "Sorry. This could've ended badly."

Matt turned his patient smile in my direction. "It's a risk I'm willing to take, little wolf. I'm proud to have such a strong, supportive mate. And this is the least I can do since you worked so hard after a horrible morning. Although he deserved what he got, I know witnessing your father's death wasn't easy."

He wasn't wrong. Despite everything my dad had done or allowed to be done to me, I'd struggled with what I'd known would happen at the end of the challenge. My father would've been first to call me weak for feeling mercy, even for my own parent. But I wouldn't be me if I didn't, and I was okay with that. Smiling back at Matt, I responded truthfully.

"No, it was no laughing matter. But given the other option? There was no contest. I will choose you every time."

"Damn straight, and it goes double for me. Not because I'm a better person than you, but I'm twice your size, so everything's automatically doubled, right?" He winked and went back to massaging my foot. "By the way, nice trick with the plants you distributed. Am I correct in assuming the existing pack members also got plants when they returned home?"

Joy burst in my chest and spread like wildfire through my veins. Realizing he already knew me so well felt good. "Obviously. Each plant was given with either a 'welcome home' or 'welcome to your new home' message, depending on the recipient. Paula oversaw distributing the 'welcome home' plants before lunch for me."

"Well, it was a thoughtful touch and a perfect use of your gift. Like I said, I'm proud to have such a strong, supportive mate. Now how about I carry you to bed? I wouldn't want you to fall down with all this slippery lotion on your precious tootsies. Once we get there, maybe we can snuggle in for a whole different kind of massage."

My dick twitched, and I shivered at the lust I both scented and felt through the bond. "If your whole different kind of massage involves the happy little trick you taught me the other day where we rub our dicks together, then sign me up and carry me away, good sir."

As his tongue slowly slid across his upper lip, Matt's eyebrow rose suggestively. "We could go over yesterday's lesson. Or I could teach you a whole new one where my tongue massages your pretty little hole. And then my fingers will join the fun while I carefully prepare you for my favorite game. You know, the one where you sit facing away and ride my cock while I buck like a bronco? After our successful day, I'm looking forward to hearing you shout 'yeehaw.'"

"Why are we still over here? I say you do less telling and more showing because this cowboy is ready to saddle up."

And since I had the best alpha in the world, that's exactly what we did.

ELEVEN

MATT

Jared and I spent the better portion of our morning going over my new financial situation. In his rush to collect pack members, Monty hadn't transferred Horace's assets over.

And as for the money tucked away in human banks, Elisha would be able to claim it as next of kin. Not everyone in our world complied with the human culture of legal marriage, but Horace made a quick trip to Vegas after taking Elisha.

Probably so he'd have a legal claim, but Jared found more than one secret bank account and a key to a safe-deposit box at a bank in Barstow—and all in Elisha's name. Tapping the key to my chin, I leaned back in the leather desk chair, here since my father was Alpha. The old springs creaked in defiance, but the chair was as solid as ever.

"Why would he risk giving Elisha a claim to his assets? I'm having trouble wrapping my brain around the idea."

Running a hand through his hair as he sighed, Jared looked weary of the whole situation. "To be honest, I think because he knew he could control Elisha and keep it hidden from the pack. At least we have the answer to the extra taxes and why no money was being spent on the town, I think. As you'll recall, Horace took all the normal overseeing duties away from the Gamma Council and left them in charge of security. The single pack member he trusted to some extent was me, and ferreting out this information he'd hidden took the better part of a week. I probably wouldn't have found everything if he didn't insist on using the same password and his bad habit of never clearing his browser history."

Growling softly, I slapped the key onto the desk. "So basically, this is all money stolen from the pack. I'll have to talk to Elisha, but I'm sure he'll agree it needs to be repaid directly to the pack's account."

Jared nodded glumly. "I'm sorry your uncle was such a bad guy. Remember, we all know you're not cut from the same cloth. This account, though, it's only in his name and hasn't been touched in a decade. He left it to accrue interest and basically forgot about it. It's the money he got from your father's accounts, so it's yours free and clear, with nothing for you to feel guilty over since you would've inherited it anyway."

"At least some good news is mixed with the bad. I have cash from odd jobs I've done over the years and an inheritance from both my mother and my grandparents. Even without taking a salary, Elisha and I would've been fine. But with these accounts, we're looking at a few million, not counting whatever is in the safe-deposit box. Once what's stolen gets repaid, the pack will be able to handle all the upcoming expenses *and* pay mine and any other overdue salaries. I'm glad we found the stash because, while I was still going to figure out a way to make it all happen, getting the town fixed up without any funding issues to consider will be much easier."

Two things happened at once, interrupting our conversation: Jared's phone rang, and someone knocked on my office door. Shrugging with a wry grin, Jared backed toward the door. "We were lucky we got this much time before being bothered." He frowned when his phone wouldn't stop ringing and answered it while opening the door. When he saw my friends, Jared stepped aside for them to enter and excused himself to take the call.

I rocked back in the chair, clasping my arms behind my head. "Come on in, gentlemen. Check out my sweet office. Try not to be jealous of its late twentieth-century flair. Uncle Horace didn't like being shut away where he couldn't keep an eye on the peasants, so it's exactly like my father left it. Except for the MacBook. Jared had it waiting when I came in here after breakfast this morning."

Whistling, Lucian made a show of grimacing at the ugly olive plaid before dusting the heavy-duty wool fabric of a guest chair which was probably older than me. He pulled it over to my desk and gingerly took a seat. "If the '70s can be considered late twentieth-century, sure. Tell me your old man left his stash of dirty magazines in one of the desk drawers, and I'll forgive his tacky decor."

Devon pulled his own chair up, aiming a narrow-eyed frown at Lucian. "Shut up, Luci. Give the man a break. You know this is his first real day sitting behind the desk. He's probably all emotional and shit, remembering the times dear old Dad called him in here for Alpha heir lessons or punishments."

"Not having had the privilege of knowing my own father, I wouldn't understand parental shit." Luci winked to take any sting out of his blunt honesty. "Still, it wouldn't hurt to get a decorator on speed dial."

Tucker didn't bother with a chair; he sat on the corner

of my desk and propped his feet on the one Jared had vacated. "Are we done dissing the man's office yet? I'm sure Matt's busier today than a one-legged man in a butt-kicking contest. He got the first round of the new pack brought in yesterday, and the rest's showing up tonight. Come on, guys. We rehearsed this, remember?"

Dropping my arms, I sat forward to show my interest. "There was a rehearsal? I'm all ears. I can't wait to hear what this is about." When they glanced uncomfortably at each other, it felt strange. "Shit. Don't get weird because I have a new job. It's hard enough to deal with all the life changes I've got happening—I need you guys to keep me normal."

Devon's gaze softened with understanding. "Sorry, Matty. It's a hard topic to broach, but here goes. We know other alphas living in a pack is unheard of, but you said you were doing things different here, right? We don't want to get a place in between here and Nick's pack. And Luci is already bitching about moving any closer to Death Valley. If you'll have us, we'd like to stay and help get your town running properly again."

The vulnerability in Lucian's eyes gutted me when he was the first to hold his wrist up. "I've never worn an alpha's mark, but I'd be proud to wear yours."

I didn't even need to consider it. "Luci, while claiming you as part of my pack would be my honor because I can't think of anyone more honorable than you or these two mofos sitting beside you—I don't want to tie any of you to me and keep you from the option of having your own pack one day. Your word is your bond, and that's good enough for me. None of you would ever rise up against me or challenge me for the pack."

Pausing to laugh at the horrified looks on their faces, finishing my thought took me a second. "I appreciate the idea, but I'm not biting any of your wrists. I welcome you to stay here and live in Lucerne Valley as long as you want. If you find a mate here and decide to remain forever, then and only then will I accept your allegiance. Until such time, you'd be considered friends of the pack, and I'll hook you up with housing since you plan to help us out anyway. What do you say—will that work for you?"

They shared a quick glance before nodding. Luci thumped a fist over his heart. "Now you went and gave me a case of feels, Matty. What a bullshit move to do to a friend." As he chuckled, his hand dropped to his lap. "Seriously, though, I'm touched. We're good with your compromise, as long as it means we get to stay together with Nick an hour's drive away."

"More like an hour and a half, if you follow the speed limit," Devon couldn't help but correct. He might have been our peacekeeper, but he also had to have the right details. Luci gave his normal response to Devon's corrections—with his middle finger raised high and proud. Tucker and I burst out laughing.

I was still catching my breath when Jared came back in. When he hesitated, I motioned for Jared to close the office door. "Come on in. You can talk freely in front of these guys. I'll end up telling them anyway." So Jared could get settled, I swatted Tucker on the ass. "I don't care if you park your mangy butt on my desk, but move your damn feet so Jared can have his chair." When Tucker responded by flipping me off, even while he dropped his feet as suggested, Jared's eyes nearly popped out of his head. Shaking my head, I grinned to put Jared at ease. "Ignore us. We've been friends for too long to pretend we have manners around each other. What's got you looking so freaked out now? Please don't tell me I have to kill someone else."

Snorting, Jared held a palm out in front of him, wavering it from side to side. "No promises on the whole killing thing. TC Woodlawn's assistant called to give us the heads-up. Rumblings are being heard throughout Southern California. Some of the alphas stuck in overcrowded areas like the LA basin have been waiting for a chance to take Lucerne Valley for their own packs. Rumor has it more than one are actively planning to come fight you so they can steal our territory. They think because you're young and new to being a pack Alpha that you'll be easy to attack, and not only will they be able to move here and have more room, but they would have a larger pack after absorbing ours."

God, I was tired. Was a peaceful life with my own pack too much to ask? Flopping my head back against the chair, I groaned up at the ceiling. "Fuck 'em. If they want to bring war to our door, I'll be ready. Arrange a meeting this afternoon with the Gamma Council. We're going to have to discuss delta patrols and pack security. This is shitty timing with everything in flux, but it is what it is." Lowering my head, I looked Jared in the eye. "What neighboring alphas might be willing to become allies? If we let the LA packs get a toehold here, theirs will be equally at risk pretty soon. If the packs in the area stand together, we'll all be stronger. Fuck the urban trash. They can stay in the cities where they belong or petition with Ash for open properties in the Central Valley. I know damn well a lot of open land up there is waiting to be had."

Tucker lifted a brow. "You're forgetting two things, Matty. First, you're a couple hours' ride from Vegas from here. Or LA, or, hell, Mexico. And secondly, you're talking farmland up in the Central Valley. Do you really think those city slickers know dick about farming? Come on, son.

Not everyone is as hardworking as we are. That's just a fact of life."

"And it's precisely why they want our pack lands." Jared nodded agreeably, drumming his fingers against the arm of his chair. I could tell he was mentally running over a list of possible allies and picturing the surrounding areas by the way his eyes shifted right and left, a lupine trait so many of us showed even in our human forms.

He finally looked back at me. "Off the top of my head, I would suggest you reach out to the alphas of the Barstow, Riverside, Mojave, and Tehachapi packs. If you call them personally, it'll be impossible for them to turn you down without looking like complete douchebags. I've met all of them, and while I wouldn't trust them any farther than I can throw them, they aren't as bad as Horace or Monty. At least, not from what I could tell. I'll forward you their numbers now." Because of course my productive beta would have contact information at his fingertips. I would expect nothing less of the man.

I couldn't help but grin when my phone dinged immediately. Taking a deep breath, I picked it up and studied the information before looking back at Jared. "Remind me of something, and please pretend I knew the information in the first place. Once I get alliance agreements, is a verbal contract enough, or do we need anything formal?"

Devon answered before Jared. "Definitely formal, Matt. The Supreme Council requires official alliance agreements be signed, notarized, and submitted to your territory chief. So you don't have people promising the moon and then letting your enemy into the back door. You can thank the Great Pack War in the 1890s. They caused so much shit back east, Chicago flooded, and both New York and Boston had fires. We were lucky the humans never discovered our existence while all that shit was going down."

Jared perked up with interest. "Didn't it all start because the New York alpha promised the New Jersey pack they'd have their back if anything happened with Long Island?" Devon was visibly excited, and the two of them geeked out on history. Tucker and Luci stood and stretched before heading toward the door. With a wry grin, Tucker glanced back over his shoulder. "Want us to drag the nerds out with us? Or can you make your calls with them yapping?"

I didn't need to answer. Jared and Devon rose and followed them out of the room without missing a beat of their conversation. Laughing softly under my breath, I steeled myself before making the first call. I wasn't sure what the reception would be, but Jared was right. If they didn't stand with me, their own packs would be at risk.

TWELVE

ELISHA

"I can't believe the businesses are already starting to reopen." Matt stared almost hungrily at a sign in the window of the Full Moon Diner. "I wish it was tomorrow. Then we could go in there and get a milkshake."

Trying not to laugh, I poked his solid stomach. "Like I thought, there's no room after your second slice of pie. And don't get me started on how many finger sandwiches I saw you putting away."

He stared at me impassively for a few seconds before blinking. "Little wolf, are you... food-shaming me? Allow me to remind you—you're the one who suggested our daily afternoon snack time."

"Emphasis on snack, my love. Not a full meal." He looked so injured. When I couldn't feel anything through the bond, I immediately felt bad. "Shoot, Matt! I didn't mean it rudely. I was teasing you. I was originally picturing snack time a little differently than what it's turned out to be, that's all."

When he started to laugh, I realized he'd been purposely closing off our bond. My mouth dropped open with an indignant huff. "You totally played me. How were you able to block me? It's a neat trick, so obviously I need to learn it immediately."

He simply laughed harder, bent over right there on the sidewalk, bracing both hands on his thighs while he brayed. Before long, I was snickering with him. Still slightly bent, he stood taller so he could look me in the eye.

"I know I'm going to regret this, but I will absolutely teach you. I wasn't sure if it would work, but I shut myself off from the pack consciousness the same way during the challenge to avoid any distractions. However… I do have one condition. First, you have to tell me how you pictured snack time going because now I think you wanted me to sit at your feet and hand-feed you or something."

Tapping my chin, I hummed slightly as the imagery washed over me. "First, we have to act your idea out sometime because it sounds sexy. But only if I get to do it for you, too. So I had pictured something more romantic. In my mind, I was sitting on your lap while we shared food from the same plate. And kissed. There were lots of kisses."

His eyes darkened as a possessive growl rumbled from his throat. "I like the way you think, little wolf. Something tells me our snack times are going to be changing. No wonder you insist on doing it in our suite. You're so subtly sneaky it's almost diabolic. My buddies would have a field day if they knew my omega was trying to seduce me while I was feeding my face."

"I suppose it all comes down to hunger and appetite either way, doesn't it?" I delivered the line so instantly Matt did a double take before cracking up again.

"Remind me never to underestimate you, Elisha. Or your planning abilities." He cupped a hand under my chin to hold my head firmly in place while he kissed me. At first it was a soft brush of lips, but then he tilted his face to plunder my mouth with his tongue. I needed several moments of passive enjoyment before I gathered myself to kiss him back.

And then I lost track of time. Nothing existed outside of Matt's mouth on mine and the large hand firmly gripping my butt. A polite throat clearing from somewhere to our left startled us apart, cheek to cheek as we glared at whoever had interrupted.

When I met Jared's amused gaze, I was horrified to realize I was completely hard, and somehow my right knee had lifted to push up against Matt's hip. My hands were locked around his neck, and I'd apparently been doing my best to climb him like a tree. On the sidewalk. In the middle of Main Street. With people working inside the shops to get them ready to open tomorrow.

Bumping my forehead against Matt's chest, I said a quiet prayer for a meteor strike. Or the ground to open and swallow me. Basically, if someone could just kill me now, that would be great.

Matt tried to soothe me over the bond, sending waves of affection and peace. Meanwhile, his hand subtly slid from my butt, gliding over my thigh to support my raised leg as if this were normal public behavior. With his cheek still pressed against mine, his smile pushed our skin closer together. When he spoke, the low timbre gave me goosebumps.

"Pardon us for disturbing whatever you wanted to say, Jared. Go on. You've got my attention." I swallowed a laugh. No one but Matt could turn a gentle rebuke for kiss-blocking us into pleasant teasing.

Jared merely lifted a brow. "Sure, Matty. I'll do my best to forgive you for being a loving alpha and proving why you were the best one for me to call in Elisha's time of need. Although I would be happy to suggest a few places offering better privacy while you share your affection. After all, you were gone for many years. It's possible you've forgotten the best makeout spots."

They stared at each other for a few seconds before Matt said, "Touché," and they both laughed. The way Jared blossomed and relaxed around Matt was amazing. Our pack beta had always seemed so stiff and formal. His own mom joked about him putting too much starch in his underwear. It could've been because Matt had a way of putting people at ease, but I figured it had a lot more to do with them growing up together.

I gave them a few moments to laugh it up before extricating myself from Matt, doing my best to seem responsible enough for a leadership role around here. It was a hard look to pull off, given I was about seven weeks or so away from giving birth and my gut had its own ZIP code these days. Put together with my elastic-fronted paternity pants and an old T-shirt of Matt's fitting me like a short dress, I didn't seem like much of an authority figure.

Whatever. The shirt's loose fabric was so soft and worn I had zero regrets. I'd liberated it from a box of old clothes packed up when he left. Paula unearthed it from somewhere and delivered it to our room this morning. The single thing missing from my new favorite shirt was Matt's scent. Although, thanks to our little display of PDA, I was definitely wearing it now.

Glancing at his watch, Jared nodded toward the road. "Everyone from Newberry Springs will be arriving soon. Were you planning to wave as they drive into town, or did you lose track of time?"

Thinking about how close they were sent a burst of

energy through me, and I wanted to bounce up and down. "Both, I guess. I want to be the first thing my brothers see when they arrive. But we might have gotten kinda distracted and forgot the time." And where we were. And pretty much everything except for each other.

Matt slipped an arm around me, his hand smoothing a circle in the small of my back. "Only a few more minutes, little wolf. I've arranged for special transportation for your brothers."

As soon as he spoke, I remembered a certain group of bikers who'd disappeared after lunch. My eyes went wide, my stomach clenching at the thought of my brothers on motorcycles. "Tell me you didn't..."

Before he could answer, the telltale rumbling of engines sounded right before three shiny bikes came into view in the distance. A wave of comfort surged through the bond, and Matt's hand still rubbed a circle against my back. Squinting to get a better look at the third bike, I had to block the sun with the back of my hand. My chest warmed as I turned to fling my arms around my mate.

"Wait. A sidecar? Please tell me nobody actually went and bought an expensive accessory to safely escort my brothers here." I stepped back and glared suspiciously. "Why aren't you telling me I'm crazy to think of such a thing?"

How had I never noticed Matt's grin could be irritating? Cute. But irritating. Even as he shrugged, he kept smiling. "Why would I call you crazy for guessing your surprise? We haven't been together long, but you already know me well enough to know the truth. And yes, Lucian did buy the sidecar. He ordered it several days ago and picked it up on the way to Newberry Springs."

Though he was still smiling, his eyes showed a hint of

concern as he shrugged again, almost nervously. "I wasn't sure what your stance was on motorcycles, especially when you've never asked for a ride. And I guess I've been afraid to ask. Lucian suggested it was probably better to beg your forgiveness later than ask permission and get shut down."

I had to roll my eyes, though I felt myself smiling. "I haven't asked because I wasn't sure I would fit with... um, all this squished up against your back." I motioned at my belly, then thrust my hand out in a wordless gesture, vaguely saying I didn't know what to think.

Matt rested his palm against the side of my gut. "You and the pup would be safe to ride with me. I don't know I would want to take you out once you get any further along. But I'm probably being protective. I knew a human woman who rode her Harley up until the day she delivered. And yes, bikes can be dangerous, but you and your brothers are safe with us. We know what we're doing. It's the other guy we have to watch out for, and none of us would ride near cars with precious cargo aboard."

Since we were talking about it, I kinda felt silly. "Plus, we *are* shifters. There's the whole benefit of fast healing we've got going for us, right? We're harder to kill." I chewed my lip as I looked back to see how close the bikes were getting. The desert played tricks on one's eyes, and sometimes gauging distance was hard. They were nearer, though, because now I could make out more details. Feeling guilty, I glanced back at Matt. "He really bought a sidecar? Specifically for this trip? For Noah to ride in?"

"Meh, don't sweat it. Luci's been quietly looking at those things for years. Devon thinks he has fantasies of getting a dog. It would be a great place for a pooch to ride. Besides, we couldn't risk him being too short. Noah's only six, you said. If he's not tall enough to ride a roller coaster, state law won't let him ride on the back of a motorcycle. Once he gets a little bigger, it won't be a problem."

As how they had put their heads together to solve my problem sank in, my chest swelled until I felt light enough to float away. "I don't know why you guys wanted to do this for me, but thank you. I'll be thanking them as well, but... yeah."

Matt lifted my chin with two fingers. "You don't have to be grateful to me for looking out for my own. Your brothers are in your care now, so they're mine too. Any of the guys' too, we take care of our family."

My vision blurred as my eyes tried to tear up. Every time I thought I had Matt figured out, he surprised me again. With everything going on, the one thing we hadn't talked about was how my brothers would fit into our life moving forward. I'd been so focused on getting them here. Realizing I hadn't given much thought to what came next surprised me. So much for my reputation as a great planner.

I gasped as they rode into town limits. Saul's long, skinny legs were pressed up against Tucker's large alpha body. I gripped Matt's arm, digging my fingers in without noticing until he gently pried them up a touch. Even then, I barely paid it much attention as I shook my head, completely sick at heart and ready to kick my own butt.

"Matt, where are they going to sleep tonight?"

I'd forgotten Jared's presence until he snorted. Leaning around Matt's back to peer at him, he greeted me with a wink. "Nobody's perfect, Elisha. While you were busy making sure the pack had housing, my mom realized you were putting yourself last and took care of it. Why do you think she was digging through Matt's old stuff? When we get back home, I think you'll be happy to find Matt's childhood bedroom is now set up with twin beds and plenty of age-appropriate toys and books."

Matt grinned as he whisper-yelled. "I might've left a present or two in there myself. As the former occupant of the room, I figured it was my duty."

Did these people not realize how emotional pregnancy could make a guy? Jared's sweet, thoughtful statement was all it took for the waterworks to start. And then Devon rolled to a stop with Lucian and Tucker following—which meant my brothers were right behind him. Noah looked adorable, sitting in the sidecar and wearing a helmet so big he might fall over if he tried to stand upright with it on.

And then I was both laughing and crying.

And basically blubbering all over myself.

And embarrassing myself in the middle of town for the second time in ten minutes.

I didn't have time to dwell on anything because everything happened so fast. The bikes shut off, and helmets were removed, and two little boys were running at me and… I didn't need to see them through my blurry, tear-filled eyes. With both arms wrapped around my brothers, their scents washed over me like a warm spring rain, soothing places in my heart I hadn't known were aching.

When I finally had a hand free, I wiped my eyes with the back of my wrist and snuffled. Noah managed to look both impressed and completely grossed out. "Eww, nasty! You need a tissue, Eli."

Saul rolled his eyes. "Be nice, pipsqueak. We haven't seen him in forever. Besides, Eli's only crying because he's happy to see us. Right, Eli?"

Looking at Saul, who was nearly as tall as me already, and Noah, who wasn't talking like a baby anymore, nearly brought me to my knees. As it hit home exactly how long we'd been apart, a wave of despair crashed into me. I took a deep breath and turned helplessly to Matt. "So... these are my brothers." It was as if someone had hit a mute button because I couldn't make myself say anything else. This whole meeting was so surreal and... poignant.

Matt paused to press a kiss against my temple before introducing himself. As I calmed, I realized my contentment was coming through the bond. Once again, Matt was looking out for me. He gave his full-watt smile to my brothers. "What's up? I'm the Alpha around here, or so they keep telling me. Mostly, I do whatever your brother says. Oh, I should probably mention I'm your brother-in-law now because Elisha is my mate."

"Is it true? Are you the one who killed our father?" Saul looked nervous but determined at the same time to know the truth.

Bless him, Matt didn't hesitate for a second. He looked my brother straight in the eye and nodded. "I did. And I hope you'll understand I won't apologize for doing it."

I don't know who was more shocked, him or me, but both boys flung their arms around Matt as if they'd known him all their lives. They were talking so fast I could barely make out what they were saying, but I distinctly heard "thank you" more than once.

Matt went to hug them back and looked to me over their heads, silently asking me how to proceed. His friend Devon solved it for us. He ruffled Saul's hair. "I take it you weren't a fan either, huh?"

Saul finally pulled away and scrubbed his eyes with both hands, somehow managing to look more like the pup I remembered than a soon-to-be teen. Gulping, he gazed at me with red-rimmed eyes. "Dad said you were dead. And when he found out you weren't, he said whoever had saved you would wish they hadn't when he killed them next, and then you'd finally die like all weak mongrels should."

Noah pressed his lips together, his little face turning red as he made fists and shook them over his head. Lucian and Tucker raised their eyebrows, but Matt quietly told him to let it out. As his lips trembled, his hands dropped, and he rushed past Matt and into my waiting arms. While I hugged him, he tearfully began to talk. "Daddy was a bad man. He hurt Scruffy and made him dead." What a bittersweet moment to hear the baby in my youngest brother again.

Matt mouthed 'Scruffy' with a questioning look. His muscles were coiled with tension, ready to battle dragons on Noah's behalf. Saul correctly interpreted Matt's confusion and translated. "Scruffy was Noah's teddy bear. Papa got it for him before he was born, and Noah always slept with it. Dad decided it was time for Noah to quit being a baby. So he..." Saul hesitated, twitching and scratching the back of his head as if delaying finishing the sentence.

After several long moments, Saul finally took a deep breath and spat it out. "He barbecued Scruffy and made Noah watch. Right on the same grill where Elisha always cooked our dinner, Dad poured lighter fluid over the bear and lit a match. When Noah cried, Dad hit him with a belt and locked him in the utility room for three days. There's water in there, and I slipped granola bars under the door. But it wasn't cool to do that to a kid Noah's age."

Looking him in the eyes, I brushed sweat-damp hair from Noah's forehead. "Saul is correct. Dad did bad things to you. It wasn't good when he did it to Saul or when he did it to me. But you know what? You never have to be afraid again. Nobody will ever hit you here or lock you in any closets. If you get in trouble, I'll make you pull weeds or something. But I want you to understand this is your home now, and Matt and I will keep you safe."

Matt rested a hand on Saul's shoulder. "Same goes for you too, big guy. I'm proud of you for looking out for Noah when he needed you most. But now I want you to relax and learn to be a kid while you still can. Your brother is my world, and if you're his family, you're mine too. Anybody who wants to hurt either one of you will have to come through me first."

"Tell the truth, Matty. Ain't nobody touching either one of these boys unless they can get through all of us." Lucian came close enough to squat down and talk to Noah. "Your new brother Matt is pack to us, and pack means family. So guess what? You and your brother inherited four honorary uncles. You've got the three of us here and Nick, the new Alpha you met at your old place. Why do you think we came and picked you up on our bikes? Because you're pack. Nobody rides with us unless they belong."

Good God in heaven. Seeing this big, broody alpha act so sweetly and say exactly what Noah needed to hear was enough to be the death of me.

I blinked back a fresh wave of tears as I fanned a hand in front of my face. If my voice was thicker than normal, nobody commented. "Matt, we need to take the kids home. Maybe get out of the heat and let them see where they live now."

"Now there's the best idea I've heard all day." Matt turned and said something to Devon. The other alpha studied me as he slowly began to grin. The next thing I knew, Matt escorted me over to Devon's bike. "It won't be the same as mine, but I can't let you be the sole member of the family who's never ridden."

Then a helmet was produced out of thin air and

plunked over my head. Matt got me settled on the back of the bike, then slipped on in front of me. I glanced around in confusion, trying to figure out what was going on.

Saul was back on Tucker's bike, while Lucian helped Noah into the sidecar. I nearly fell off the bike when Devon quietly climbed on behind Lucian.

Once again, all I could think was... alphas weren't supposed to be like this. Matt's pack of alphas blew every stereotype I'd ever heard right out of the water. I might've dwelled on the concept longer, but every thought in my head blinked out of existence, and it was all I could do to grab Matt and hold on tight when the engine rumbled to a start.

And the vibrations! I had to clamp my teeth together to keep them from rattling against each other. I was pretty sure my insides were rearranging themselves. Was shaken baby syndrome possible in utero?

I was about to beg Matt to forget the whole thing and let me get off when the bike moved. Jared stood on the sidewalk, smiling as he held up his phone to take a picture. I started to playfully flip him off but thought better of it when I realized I'd have to let go of Matt.

Besides, I didn't need to look like a tough biker. All I had to do was hang on tight to the one I had. Both literally and figuratively. Whatever. I was holding on to my man.

My belly was a hard ball wedged in between us, but I leaned over it and squeezed both arms as snugly as I could around Matt's waist. When he revved the engine and took off with a burst of speed, a wave of sheer happiness spread through me as we sped toward home.

It was like nothing I'd ever experienced. Whenever I'd ridden in a car, I always enjoyed watching the scenery go by when I looked out the window. But now, I was part of the scenery. One with the landscape. Completely immersed and united with the world around us, nothing between me and nature. My grip loosened as I began to relax, and by the time we came to a stop, I was disappointed the ride had ended.

After our helmets were off, the first thing Matt did was kiss me hard and fast. His eyes were like liquid gold when he pulled back to ask what I thought of the ride. I was finally able to let out the giggles I'd been holding in. My happiness swirled around us like a living thing as I laughed with sheer joy.

"What did I think? It was the best! Glorious. Amazing, even. And when can I go again?"

I hadn't heard the other guys pull up; I'd been too focused on my mate and the intense exhilaration of my first ride. So focused, in fact, I nearly jumped out of my skin when the other alphas chuckled.

Lucian tipped his chin toward me in approval. "Spoken like a true member of the family. Welcome to the pack, Elisha. You already were one of us 'cuz of Matty boy, but now you belong all on your own."

We were all still standing around the bikes as Jared drove up. When I saw the stream of cars following him, I turned to Matt. "We forgot to greet the new and returning pack members. I feel awful."

Matt caught my hand and lifted it to kiss my inner wrist. "You don't need to feel bad for a second, little wolf. Jared was there to greet everyone. There is nothing improper about the pack beta doing the initial hello. You had to take time and greet the two people who matter most, and you did. Now how about we take the boys inside and show them their new bedroom? If memory serves, Paula has the whole dinner buffet thingy planned in the old ballroom so we don't have much time."

"Remind me never to doubt you, my love. You're right. Let's take more family time and check out the boys' new digs."

By the time we made it inside, Paula was already hugging Noah and Saul. Jared headed off with his clipboard to direct our incoming pack members to the community room—or old ballroom, if you were Matt. By the time Paula let my brothers go, they both had somehow wound up with cookies in their hands, and Paula shot me a look daring me to question it.

I smothered a laugh and pointed my brothers toward the stairs. If she wanted to spoil them, more power to her. As a fellow survivor of my father's house, I could vouch for how much pampering they had to make up for. And since I would need them to respect me, it was probably better if a grandma type did it.

Exactly like Jared said, a pair of twin beds had been installed in the bedroom closest to our suite. And toys. And books. And a lot of empty drawers and closet space, ready to be filled with new clothes. When Noah spotted a friendly teddy bear propped up against the pillow on one of the beds, he raced over and snatched it up. While he hugged his new treasure, I heard a suspicious sniffle. Four blinking alphas were obviously battling an acute allergic response of some sort.

When I caught Matt watching intently as Saul trailed a fingertip over a new cellphone box on his own pillow, I remembered his comment about leaving a gift or two as the room's former occupant. Elbowing him in the ribs, I tried not to laugh at his expression as I shot him a playful glare. "Am I correct when I think you bought a cellphone for a twelve-year-old?" Since I couldn't block—yet—I knew the second he felt my amused affection through our bond. His expression switched from guilt to pride in a heartbeat.

"Hey, what can I say? I was worried he might have friends back in Newberry Springs he'd want to stay in touch with. Plus, there's so many other things you can do with phones. You know, like take pictures, listen to music, and read books and... I don't know, Google shit? Yeah, I figured it was a good welcoming gift. Like your plants? Same difference. It's a little thing to make him smile."

I snorted so hard my nose tickled. "You gave him the latest iPhone. I don't even have that model. Are we seriously comparing phones to plants?"

Shrugging, Matt held his hands out, shoving his cheek against a shoulder with a wry grin. "It's a fair comparison. Don't forget, it *is* an Apple product. If we can't compare apples to plants, then I don't know what to tell you."

Our fun continued all through dinner, especially when Noah found out we were having spaghetti. We tried to avoid carb-heavy meals back home, especially this time of year. Mostly because my father didn't approve of air-conditioning. He said it wasn't natural, but I always thought it had more to do with him being cheap. Spaghetti was a winter treat, while lean proteins and salads were standard fare the rest of the year. Unlike back home, though, our solar-powered manor was kept cool enough to eat whatever the heck we wanted. And to prove it, I pretended not to notice when Noah overdid it on the garlic bread.

Once we were done with dinner, Matt gave the same speech he'd given twice before. After welcoming everyone to the pack and letting them know what to expect, we made our way around the room for his final round of wrist biting, accepting the allegiance of this final round of pack members to arrive. Initiation over, Jared and a team of volunteers left to take everyone to their new homes. At least the ones who didn't already have family here waiting for them.

Once everyone was gone except for us and the alpha crew, the guys made noises about heading to town to see if anyone needed help. We were about to say goodbye and head upstairs with the boys when Paula bustled in with a tray filled with big bowls of strawberry ice cream. She took one look at us and sternly shook her head. "Nope. Jared rushed everyone out of here before I got to serve dessert. These young boys need a treat, and the rest of you do too."

Already licking his lips, Tucker grabbed for a bowl. "Strawberry? Count me in. You got any chocolate syrup to pretty it up, darlin?"

Giggling like a schoolgirl, Paula set the tray in the middle of the table and produced a bottle of Hershey's syrup from her apron. "Better watch your flirty smile, young man. My boyfriend might have a few years on you, but he's an excellent shot." She winked to let him know she was teasing, but Tucker simply grinned harder.

"Ma'am, after tasting your cooking, I'm willing to risk the wrath of anyone if it'll get me an extra helping of whatever you're serving. Especially if he's not smart enough to have you claimed by now."

Paula waved him off. "Oh, you. Behave or I'm putting you on dishwashing duty. And who wants a claim at my age? I had my mate, and I loved him to pieces. These days I can have fun sharing a few moonlight kisses without having to worry about anyone hogging the covers later. Now you boys enjoy your treat. I've got to check on my kitchen staff and make sure everything is running on schedule."

While we ate dessert, Matt told me about some alliances in the works with neighboring packs. Surprisingly, he brought it back around to the sign he'd stared at in the diner window earlier, mentioning his plans to have lunch there with some strange alpha.

"I told him it would have to wait until next week because my schedule was jam-packed right now. But yeah, the Tehachapi alpha wants to meet me in person before he signs an official alliance agreement."

Lucian wagged a finger. "I don't like it, bro. Less than an hour after you started making calls, you had ally agreements locked in with everyone but him and that Barstow dick wouldn't even take your call. What makes this dude thinks he's so special? I think he wants to come scope the place out, if you ask me."

Matt seemed to consider the idea before sighing. "You're not saying anything I didn't think of myself at the time. Hell, after I talked to the San Bernardino pack, the Alpha from Baker reached out on his own. They all seem wary but willing to give it a shot. They know as well as we do: if the LA packs get a toehold out here, everyone in the area is in danger of the same shit we are."

Noah interrupted, his stern expression completely ruined by the pink ice cream covering half his cute face and the entire front of his shirt. "You said a bad word, Matt. You're gonna get in trouble with Eli."

My cheeks were on fire. "When I lived in Newberry Springs, I kept a swear jar to keep people from cursing in front of the boys. It never stopped our father, but it helped everyone else tone it down. And whenever the jar got full, I treated the boys to ice cream. The bribe is probably what made Noah notice. Please don't think you have to police your language on my account—I don't personally mind. Especially because Noah is old enough to know the difference between what he hears from grown-ups and the words he's allowed to say."

Setting his spoon down, Matt leaned over to kiss my cheek. "Start the swear jar, little wolf. There is a new pup on the way, and we might as well start learning to watch our language now."

"Ahh... erm... this is only around little ones, right? We can talk however we want if there's only adults in the room?" Poor Lucian could barely get his questions out; he truly appeared about to panic. But then again, I didn't know him well enough to guess if he was teasing or not.

In case he really was worried, I nodded quickly to set him at ease. "Only around the kids, Lucian. I don't care how you guys talk when you're alone."

Lucian made a show of wiping nonexistent sweat from his forehead with the back of his hand. "Whew. I thought for sure I was gonna go broke within a year."

Rolling my eyes, I threw a napkin at him before turning back to Matt. "I missed at least half of the story when you told me about the need for allies during snack time earlier. My mind was on other things. I've got the gist, though, so tell me what's up with this Tehachapi Alpha. You say he's coming here next week?"

"Yeah, I don't want to get everyone alarmed. He could just be nosy. My family has a long history in this valley, so you'd think it would grant me immediate acceptance. But then again, my story is perfect for the gossip mill, I suppose. I did walk away from my birthright a decade ago and came rushing back to save you, only to discover you're my true mate. And then I topped it off by challenging and killing your father."

I grimaced as understanding settled in. "And to make matters worse, you didn't keep the spoils of the challenge.

You unselfishly gave the pack away to another Alpha who would have time to properly focus on his own pack, while you were content to keep the pack which should have been yours in the first place. Huh. Yep, I can see where gossip is probably spreading like wildfire."

Tucker chuckled softly. "You both left out the best part. He also considers himself part of an exclusive all-alpha biker pack. Oh, yeah. Our Matty boy is going to be legendary around these parts."

Matt groaned and got distracted by his ice cream. When he finally set his spoon down, he pushed his half-finished bowl aside. "So like I said, I don't know. Could be something, could be nothing. Either way, I put his visit off for a week so I could get a feel for the pack deltas and how well they function as a team. The diner is reopening, so I'll take him there for lunch next week."

I rested my hand over his. "Makes sense. Good call not bringing him to our home when you don't know if you can trust him. The public diner is an excellent spot, and the deltas will have no problem watching your back with all those windows. No offense to you guys because you're different. But there's a reason Alpha stereotypes exist and why most alphas don't traditionally hang out with each other."

Devon smiled sadly in agreement. "Unfortunately, most other alphas can't be trusted. Not only do they think owning whatever catches their eye is their right, you have to worry about getting bit in the *a*—butt with alpha venom. You saw for yourself how fast it works. At least the mating bite has a chance of survival. Pure alpha venom? Not a chance."

"True that." Matt tried his best to appear positive, and it worked for everyone who couldn't feel his tension through the bond we shared. Rolling his shoulders back, he held his hands out expressively. "How scared can I be of a guy named Bart Macklebee the Third? He claims he's got a small, wealthy pack and needs to think of their needs before committing to anything. Who knows? I decided to take a measured risk."

Lucian frowned thoughtfully, waving his pointer finger as if trying to remember something. His eyes brightened. "Tehachapi. I remember why the name sounded so familiar —the speed trap on the highway between Bakersfield and Mojave. Rich little town up in those hills, remember? I couldn't believe what they were asking for a pack of gum. I noticed a lot of grapes growing in the area. If they're vintners, it would explain why he's so paranoid about outsiders."

"I had the same take too. It's why I decided to take his request at face value. As long as I can get the pack to go about their business and the deltas are ready for anything, we should be fine. We'll get the word out—I want him to leave here with the picture of a small, friendly pack. Then I'll get his signature on an ally agreement, and we'll have one more wall of defense between us and LA."

As conversation shifted back to easier topics, Noah interrupted again when Matt said something about how big the pack consciousness was now. He was in the middle of describing the way it felt to be aware of so many wolves when Noah climbed up beside him. Matt stopped mid-sentence to give Noah his complete attention. "What's up, little dude? You have something on your mind?"

In response, Noah wriggled as he pulled his shirt over his head and dropped it to the floor. I was torn between nervous laughter and wondering what the heck had gotten into him when Noah pointed at the pale scratch mark over his heart. "If all the kids belong to their parents, and they belong to you because you bited their wrists, who gets me now? And Saul?"

Matt treated Noah's question with the solemnity it deserved. "I see. You saw me accept the allegiance of all the grown-ups earlier. And you know the kids don't have to be claimed because they belong to their parents. Yes, I can see where you might worry. Even though I told you Elisha and I will take care of you now, you don't feel like you're part of the pack because you don't have a parent who's sworn allegiance to me."

I'm not sure how much of Matt's adult response went over his head, but Noah got the gist of it. Head bobbing up and down, he tapped his scar again. "Me and Saul can't be part of the pack conscience. That's not fair."

"Consciousness, little dude. *Conscience* is a completely different word." Matt gently corrected Noah while we shared a long look, love flowing through our bond as I understood his intention. Glancing at Saul, Matt traced a fingertip over Noah's scar. "Your brother is right. I can protect you, but in order for you to truly be pack and bonded to us, I'd need to give you both a sire-claiming scratch. How do you feel? Would it feel weird to be considered my kids if I'm barely old enough to be your father and am technically your brother-in-law? To be clear, you can still call me Matt. I'm not asking to become your parent, but I would assume the rights of one and be able to completely protect you."

I wasn't surprised when Saul didn't need time to think about it. Saul's gift was more empathic than mine. He couldn't read minds psychically, but he felt their intentions and emotions, and was somehow able to know what people were up to. His gift was growing and would continue to for the next few years, but it was already strong enough to trust when faced with a decision like this.

I wasn't sure Saul was old enough to completely understand how much faith he was giving Matt if he did this. And if it was anyone other than Matt, I would find a way to prevent it. But my mate would never sell or barter my brothers because they happened to be omegas. Claiming them as his own was the ultimate active protection because nobody would ever be able to get away with hurting them unless, like my father, he allowed it to happen.

When Saul pulled off his own shirt as he walked over to stand beside Matt, my heart swelled with pride. And to be honest, I felt a certain amount of relief as well. Now we truly would be one family.

Matt didn't make a big deal out of it or act like he was behaving better than any decent person. Starting with Saul, he extended a single claw and drew an X over the original scar. His sharp claw broke the flesh and removed all traces of my father's mark while claiming Saul as his own pup to protect. Noah leaned out of the way and wrinkled his nose when Matt sealed it by licking the wound. When he was done, Matt stuck his tongue out to show it was clean while tickling Noah under the chin. "I know, little man. It's gross, but we're wolf shifters, and sometimes gross things are part of life." He winked, then turned and held his arms out to Saul.

I don't think there was a dry eye around the table while my gangly brother hugged his new Alpha. As soon as they were done, Noah tugged on Matt's shirtsleeve. "My turn! Me next, remember?"

Chuckling, Matt held up his claw. "Like I could ever forget about you. Are you ready? I don't know if it stings. I was a baby when I got mine."

"Me too!" Noah trembled with excitement and proudly stuck his chest forward. "Don't worry, Matt. I'm no baby. I won't cry."

Matt took a moment to keep from laughing. I could feel how much he loved my brothers, and I knew it would be the same when I gave birth.

Resting a hand on Noah's shoulder, Matt paused before opening the scar. "I need you to hold still, Noah. My claw is very sharp, and I would be sad if I cut you too deep. Even if we got you healed right up, it would make me cry. You don't want to make a grown alpha cry, do you?"

Noah's eyes were wide as he shook his head. "No, Matt. I can behave, see?" His cheeks puffed out as he took a deep breath and struggled to hold his body motionless.

"For the love of God, man. Mark the child before he passes out." Lucian was visibly fighting his own emotions.

When Matt finally broke Noah's scar, Noah's breath came out in a whoosh as he giggled. "That tingles, Matt. It feels like magic."

Fortunately, Matt worked quickly, adjusting for my brother's wiggling. He was done in a matter of seconds and already licking the scar. Noah scrunched his nose, probably about to point out how nasty the practice was all over again, when a look of wonder passed over his face instead.

"Matt! It *is* magic! I can feel you in my heart, and I love you too." I couldn't help it—I started crying the moment Matt pulled Noah onto his lap and hugged him.

Lucian ruffled Saul's hair. Sniffling and wiping his nose on the back of his hand, he stepped away, motioning for Tucker and Devon to follow. When he saw me watching, Lucian shrugged. "Dang hay fever. I need to look into finding some medication or something. I'm heading to town.

Come on, you two, let's give these guys some time to settle in as a family."

After they left, Saul shot me a knowing look. "You do know he wasn't really suffering from allergies, right? He was proud of Matt and happy for us. I'm glad Lucian is part of our family. He needs to know people love him."

Matt looked startled when Saul finished. "Wow. A dead-on description of Lucian. How did you catch all that at twelve? I knew the guy for three years before I figured half of it out."

Blushing, Saul looked down at the table and shrugged. "What can I say? It's a gift."

Matt did a double take and looked at me curiously. "I'm not going to ask, but should I assume this is related to your green thumb?"

Smiling softly, I shook my head. "Can't answer. Not mine to tell."

Saul rolled his eyes in the world-weary way no one but a twelve-year-old could pull off. "Don't talk in riddles, Eli. You're not Confucius, and Matt isn't Dad. If he was, I wouldn't be wearing his mark now." He stood and stacked dirty ice cream bowls. "And Matt? The answer is yes. It's exactly like Eli's green thumb."

THIRTEEN

MATT

After I put them through their paces, the pack deltas didn't need much training to get where I wanted them. On the whole, they were good wolves who didn't have a problem taking orders. Exactly what was needed for a solid security system.

When Bart Macklebee the Third rolled into town in his shiny white Cadillac Escalade, he never saw the wolves I had patrolling in the background or the sharpshooters placed in strategic positions.

Having both human and wolf deltas working together wasn't exactly traditional, but I wasn't exactly a traditional alpha. And when at least a quarter of my deltas served in the human military, I'd be an idiot not to take advantage of their skills.

In addition to them, I had deltas stationed outside of every business. When Bart got out of his car and glanced around over the rim of his pricey sunglasses, I took a moment to get a read on him.

His loose-fitting, navy-colored slacks were designer and definitely not of the standard poly-cotton blend fabric most of us wore around here. He wore a white polo with the sleeves of a red sweater tied around his neck, the body hanging behind him like a preppy version of a cape.

As a gust of hot wind blew past him, the sweater fluttered in the breeze, but his perfectly styled blond hair didn't move. I took my time walking over, letting him feel my power before I got close so he wouldn't feel threatened.

"Bart Macklebee the Third, I presume? I'm Matt Longclaw. Welcome to Lucerne Valley." From a distance, I'd clocked him at about thirty, but closer, I realized he was closer to forty. Botox might fix a lot of things, but there wasn't much a man could do about how the tender flesh of the neck showed age faster than anything.

I wouldn't know yet, since I was still a couple years away from thirty. But my observational skills had been honed over a lifetime. To my point, before accepting the hand he stuck out, I knew it was going to be lotion-soft and not the grip of any kind of farmer I'd ever met.

He smiled as we shook hands, more of a grimace, actually, but damned if those perfect white teeth didn't almost blind me. "Alpha Longclaw, it's a pleasure to meet you. Your town is charming. I like the way you're spread out here. Maybe one day we can return the favor, and I can treat you to lunch in my town. It's beautiful, but those mountains can make a man feel closed in at times. Especially when it snows."

Chuckling internally, I released his hand and motioned for the diner. "I wouldn't know much about snow. Around here, we have two temperatures. Hot or wet. If it's not raining, the sun shines hard until it's hotter than Satan's taint. The rain's not much better. A good storm will wash out our roads, and the ground is too dry to soak it in, so we have to worry about flooding. But enough griping about the weather. Let's head inside and get something to drink."

I nodded at the delta casually leaning against the wall, who didn't move until our approach. Even then, it was to open the door before he went back to his leaning post. I knew because we'd planned it.

As we walked inside, Bart removed his sunglasses, shoving them up onto his head. I could only imagine what kind of impression the scarred, peeling linoleum and cracked vinyl in the booths made on the man. Like the rest of the town, the place would need time to get fixed up, but at least it was able to reopen in the meantime.

To his credit, he didn't seem to be sticking his nose up. He plucked a laminated menu card from the hostess stand, where a sign instructed us to seat ourselves. Taking one for myself, I followed him as he passed the other patrons and led me to the farthest table, where we might have a modicum of privacy.

After we took our seats on opposite sides of the booth, he looked around some more, taking in the faded, '50s-era posters and old records nailed to the back wall and over the tables. He didn't look back at me until after fidgeting with the broken tabletop jukebox. "Shame. I love these retro diners. I'm a sucker for listening to the tabletop juke." His eyes widened, and he laughed as he tapped one of the song titles on the broken machine. "'Ain't That a Shame,'" he read off with a grin. "I love finding poetic justice in the universe. It's like the machine knows it's a shame she disappointed me today."

I dropped my guard enough to smile, curiously tilting my head to the side. "*She?* Are we assigning gender to our jukeboxes now?"

"Of course. What else but a female would take perverse

pleasure by taunting a desperate man who needed his fix of classic rock 'n roll?"

While I found his joke sexist, his logic amused me. We made small talk as we perused our menus and waited for our waitress to come take the order. Since I'd always found a good way to judge a person was how they treated people serving them, I was impressed when he took the time to read Cindy's name tag and be polite before placing the order.

When it was my turn, I was barely able to maintain a poker face as she unknowingly blurted the one secret I didn't want Bart or any other neighboring alphas to know. It was like having an out-of-body experience. I was both watching and experiencing it at the same time while Cindy innocently smiled and told me how cute the First Mate's two little omega brothers were.

Keeping an easy smile on my face, I thanked her and got my order in before she gave anything else away. Like what bedroom window needed to be breached to find them in the night. I couldn't blame the girl; this was on me. I was so concerned about keeping their existence on the down-low. My mistaken logic had been if I didn't make a big deal out of it, people would be less likely to gossip or say something in front of the wrong person.

Bart was instantly fascinated. "Forgive me. I can well imagine why you probably don't want your family to become public knowledge. So when you claimed your mate to save him from the infamous lover's poison and then challenged his father, you ended up with not one, but three omegas. Good God, man. It's like having access to your own personal harem. No wonder Monty kept his pack to himself out there in that godforsaken desert. He didn't dare let anyone know what kind of treasures he was hiding under his own roof."

Thankfully, Cindy appeared with two cups of coffee, saving me from having to respond. I forced myself to calm down and ignore the harem comment, focusing on opening sugar packets and creamers and mixing them into my drink.

Apparently, Bart wasn't able to read the room because he blithely continued talking about my family. I might have convinced myself to ignore his ignorance if he hadn't pushed the issue. "All kidding aside, are you considering yet what you might ask for their dowries in the future? Depending on their ages, I'd like time to move some money around and be able to prepare before you start accepting bids."

The single sign of my disgust was my cup clattering against the saucer as I set it back down. Keeping a smile firmly in place, I took a calming breath. "No, I haven't started thinking about dowries because I don't plan on taking bids for those boys' futures. In my book, an omega is to be protected, and I intend to. Both boys aren't anything but kids who need a loving home. They're my family now, and I refuse to think about either of them as a commodity."

Bart's eyes went wide as he held both palms up. "No worries, my friend. I hope we haven't got off on the wrong foot—I've merely never had the opportunity to add an omega to my pack. Forgive me if I offended you. I was mostly curious."

Things smoothed over after I accepted his apology, and our conversation turned to why an alliance between our packs would be mutually beneficial. By the time he left, I had a signed and notarized ally agreement—thanks to a quick stop at the newly reopened pawn shop a few doors down, also offering notary services. Once Bart rolled out of sight, Tucker slipped from the shadows and came over to ask how things had gone.

I simply shook my head and held out the document. "Everything went according to plan. Once this gets sent over to Ash's office, it'll be official."

Tucker stared after the departing taillights. "And him? Anything we need to worry about?"

"I'm not sure. On the surface, he seems friendly and easygoing enough. But I didn't like a couple of the jokes he made. What kind of grown-ass alpha wants to know about a future dowry for a child?"

FOURTEEN

ELISHA

I WAS in my favorite position: facing Matt's knees, squatting over his cock while he bucked his hips. Matt had a firm grip on my shoulders, pulling me down every time he thrust upward.

It wasn't necessary; I wanted this perfectly symbiotic moment as badly as he did. Need coiled in my gut as lightning spread through my rubbery limbs. Gripping his legs, I bounced faster, meeting him stroke for stroke with each undulating pump.

It was so close, my perfect release to make me see stars and leave me floating in ecstasy. By this point, we were both drenched in sweat, but we weren't slowing down. The muscles in my legs screamed at me to kneel rather than squat.

My muscles could shut up because I loved the control planting my feet on either side of my man's body gave me. I let my head roll back. My hair had been growing so fast recently; it tickled the tops of my shoulders as I rolled my head from side to side.

I sucked in a deep breath, my nostrils flaring as I took in

the sweet, musky smell of our sex. His knot thickened and pressed against my magical place, sending electrical pulses straight to my balls and causing me to gasp for air. Jerking forward, I gave in to the impulse to lick the sweat from the inside of his knee.

It wouldn't be long now. The waves of orgasm curled up, preparing to crash. My balls were so tight they ached, and it would only take a stroke or two with a tight grip around my dick to have me shooting like a star. A porn star, I mean.

But I wanted to get off without touching myself, for Matt's knot to fill me. Fill me so good and full I would be stretched to my limits, while his fat knot pushed against my happy spot and milked the cum right out of me.

I tried to keep the rhythm going, but my aching legs were already betraying me. When the knot I was so hungry for became impossibly thick, I could barely keep moving when a universe of glittery stars shot across my closed eyelids.

It was glorious. Amazing. It was... oh, *fuuuuuck*. It was almost too much. When I faltered, Matt's rough hands sent a fresh wave of goosebumps over my quivering flesh, sliding down along my back before firmly gripping my hips.

Trying hard not to scream with pleasure, I drew blood biting into my lip. Matt's fat knot grew until pulling out was impossible. His hands jolted me back and forth like a puppet, grinding my ass on his knot.

My fists clenched so tight my nails dug half-moons into my palms. Boneless, I started to let go, falling back as Matt came forward. He sat up all the way, catching me against his broad chest without missing a move.

His arms rested around my waist, right over my belly, and I settled my arms over his, squeezing his hands and grunting as I rocked. *So close.* My eyes shut again, clenching so I saw a whole different type of stars—white shadows, transposed over the same glittery universe.

"Please." I didn't know what I was asking for, but whatever it was, I needed it badly. The one thing to push me over the edge and straight into ecstasy. *"Need."* I pushed my desperation at Matt through the bond, silently begging for the release I knew he could give me.

"Shh, little wolf. I've got you. Your alpha knows what you need." Since I trusted him so completely, his words were a balm to my frazzled nerves. I let my head roll back against his shoulder, turning to look away while I gave my body the freedom to feel. To live in the moment and enjoy the ride.

Like a roller coaster, everything built to this moment, and we were about to crest the ridge, plummeting us straight down through pure exhilaration. Matt nuzzled my exposed neck, his nose bumping against my claiming scar.

"Yesssss..." That. More of that. As his hot silky tongue slowly lapped over the mark he'd put there, goosebumps broke out all over my body. But then—oh, fuuuck—but then his teeth scraped over the scar, and my throat opened as a triumphant howl escaped. I felt completely at one with my wolf, and my mate, and the entire natural world.

My toes curled, clutching the blankets as my body stiffened before I finally found my elusive but necessary release. A white-hot lightning bolt shot down my spine and straight to my balls. It erupted from my aching dick in pearly streaks of cum, landing on my legs, surprisingly cool against my flushed, overheated skin.

To see them, I'd have to turn and open my eyes—neither of which I was willing to do at the moment. Matt licked another stripe over my scar, and I nearly came unglued, jerking and shaking in his arms as if holding a live wire. His knot stretched to its maximum girth, jamming against my overly sensitized nerve bundle and milking a second orgasm from me.

My reserves were spent; nothing else was coming out anytime soon. My balls clenched, and my body didn't know whether to laugh or cry at the strange, tickling sensation inside them. My dick gave a valiant twitch, and an almost painful shock pulsed in the center where cum should've spurted free.

When Matt shot inside of me, it was both amazing and irritating enough to make me envious. He felt something in the bond. As he rolled us onto our sides to catch our breath and snuggle until his knot released, he had to ask.

"What was the flash of jealousy I felt at the end there, little wolf?" When I was silent for too long, he playfully pinched my nipple. Groaning through a laugh, I batted his hand away. He changed his method of attack and nipped at my earlobe instead. His hot breath fanning over my ear would've got me going again if my dick wasn't so completely spent. His normally sexy chuckle wasn't doing anything for me either. "Come on, tell me what's going on inside your beautiful brain."

Well, crap. Now I felt petty. I twisted and craned my neck so I could see his face. "Promise not to laugh? I was right in the middle of coming. I mean, I just finished, but my body was still orgasmic when your knot milked a dry come out of me, I think. It was weird, but it tickled, but hurt and felt good, but burned and... then you came, and I was resentful you could while I was totally drained. Am I a selfish lover?"

Feeling his smug pride without even looking at the accompanying smirk, I wanted to roll my eyes. "Not at all.

I've had a dry come before—shit isn't fun. Everything leading up to the final moment is, but... yeah. It's a weird mix of so good and horribly wrong at the same time. And no, you're not a selfish lover. You only could be if you cared about getting off without making sure I did too. I think a better description would be to say you had cum envy, you greedy little thing."

Snickering, I couldn't help but agree. "You're not wrong. It is greedy to be jealous of you coming when my first load was fresh." We stared at each other for a second, then burst out laughing. Then we were awkwardly kissing, thanks to the position we were currently stuck in. When we rested against the pillows, I ran my fingertips lightly along his arm where it lay over my stomach. "I love you so much, Matt. That was amaaazing. You literally fucked me into a dry come."

"I love you too. And can I add I am liking the dirty mouth you're developing in the bedroom?"

My first reaction was to feel guilty and calculate how much I owed the swear jar. But then I remembered the loophole and glanced over my shoulder with a teasing grin. "I'm glad you like it. I'm happy this is one place I don't have to worry about tender ears overhearing anything they shouldn't."

Chuckling again, Matt kissed my shoulder. "I'm just hoping the sexy little howl you gave off toward the end there didn't wake them up."

I was midway through a drowsy yawn when a loud crack of thunder rumbled overhead, and our curtains glowed from the bright white bolt of lightning lighting up the sky. Snuggling back against Matt, I was about to say something about how close the storm had to be if there was no separation between the thunder and lightning. I didn't have to when rain started slamming the windows so hard it sounded like rocks hitting the glass.

Sighing softly, Matt rested his chin on my shoulder. "I wish I could take comfort in a good summer rainstorm like I would if we were up north. This won't do anything to help California's drought. At least not in our neck of the woods. We'll be lucky if we don't have flooding, but we'll definitely have to contend with a lot of mud tomorrow. Those unpaved roads are going to be riddled with clumps and ridges which will dry like cement. I'll have to use a grader to smooth everything out and make it drivable again. Unless I get lucky and it passes before people start driving around and screwing the roads up in the first place."

Smiling into the darkness, I loved discovering something my normally positive mate could get grumpy about. How an otherwise innocuous summer storm irritated him this much was particularly amusing.

A little while later, I was caught somewhere in the odd place of neither completely awake nor asleep when Matt carefully slipped out of me, his knot finally deflated. He murmured something about cleaning us before crawling out of bed and slipping into the bathroom. I had enough energy to muster a weary smile when he came back a few seconds later—or maybe hours, who could tell? Not me. While the storm raged outside our windows, I was slipping into a place where time had no meaning.

My eyes drifted shut, and sleep pulled me under. I gratefully fell to its sweet embrace, only to snap awake almost immediately when Matt started dressing me in pajama pants like a life-size baby doll. Blinking drowsily, I yawned and tried to coherently ask what the hell was going on, but what came out was something like, "whaaamazzittflp."

A few yawns later, his lips brushed over mine when he climbed back into bed. "Sorry to disturb your sleep, little wolf. The entire time we were knotted together, or at least the part after the storm came up out of nowhere, I couldn't stop worrying about Noah coming to find one of us if he got scared and accidentally getting answers for sex questions he's too young to even be curious about yet. Sure, he might ask where babies come from, but he has no reason to wonder about knots. Dear God, all I could think was I would be responsible for traumatizing our little man forever."

As badly as I wanted to laugh, he wasn't wrong, and I definitely didn't want either one of my brothers to stumble in here and find us naked and stuck together in our post-coital bliss. I woke up enough to mutter. "If they did, I'm pretty sure I'd be the one traumatized forever. But do you know how much I love you for worrying about it?" I turned and rolled over into his embrace. Almost instantly, all thoughts of disturbed brothers and the horror of being on display drifted away as sleep claimed me.

It felt like no time had passed when a particularly loud clap of thunder jolted me awake. Almost immediately, our bedroom door flew open so fast it banged into the wall. Luckily, I was aware enough to avoid being trampled when a completely terrified Noah scrambled onto the bed and dove right in between us with his new best friend Luci-boo the bear tucked firmly in the crook of his left arm. I groaned and winced as bony elbows and knees, not to mention one badly timed heel, rammed into soft tissue and vulnerable places I'd been too sleepy to defend. It took me a few seconds, but I was wide awake as I brushed a kiss over his forehead.

"This isn't going to become a habit, but I'll give you a

free pass during thunderstorms. Especially since Matt was already halfway expecting your arrival."

Hugging the bear to his chest, Noah rubbed one of Luci-boo's ears between a thumb and forefinger while he turned toward Matt. "Really? You're not mad I came into your room while you were sleeping?"

Matt snuggled his face beside Noah's and put his arm around both of us. "Do I look mad, little man? I told you I was here to take care of you, didn't I? My protection definitely includes thunderstorms. But next time, maybe you should knock first. I wouldn't want you to be embarrassed if one of us was getting dressed or something."

Noah's body shook with laughter as he giggled into his teddy bear's fur. He was saying something, but I couldn't quite make it out. Probably for the best since it sounded like he was amused at the idea of seeing my naked heinie.

We finally got Noah calmed down and were drifting back towards sleep when another loud clap of thunder sounded, so close the windows rattled. Once again, such an amazing show of lightning followed, lighting up the entire room like we'd turned on a lamp. In under a minute, a second thunderous boom shook the house, and I lifted my head at the sound of running feet.

I waited for the lightning to brighten the room, surprised when Saul appeared, barely inside. He braced against the open door with his palms pressing into the wood. He showed no sign of coming closer, despite his heaving chest and the deer-in-the-headlights expression on his face. Thankfully, we had a very large bed. I patted the empty space beside me and invited him to join us.

"Come on, Saul. Don't stand there staring at us like a creeper. Climb in and we'll sleep in a big puppy pile. Apparently, Matt thinks we do this during thunderstorms."

To help Saul save face, I tried to sound nonchalant to the point of appearing I wasn't into it. It hardly mattered when the kid could feel my true, loving concern, and every single one of us knew it.

Saul crept closer, obviously discreetly sussing out Matt's reaction to his presence. Matt lifted his hand and pointed toward my side of the bed. "You heard your brother—get in here. Puppy pile for the win."

As he pulled back the blankets and carefully climbed in beside me, Saul tried to play it cool. "Sure, since you guys seem to want me so bad. I came to check on Noah. I wanted to make sure he was okay."

I forced myself to avoid the temptation to tease him. And though I thought about it, I didn't even allow myself to point out he was reenacting the scene from *The Sound of Music* when the kids all ended up in Maria's bed. Instead, I turned and kissed his cheek, grinning when he grimaced. For his sass, I ruffled his hair for good measure. "Good night, pipsqueak. Love you."

The sweet siren call of sleep called my name, and I went willingly, without a fight. Right as I was about to drift completely under, Noah spoke up in a voice far too chipper to be ready for bed. "I like puppy pile sleepovers. We should do this again and again."

When Matt chuckled, I had to force myself awake long enough to nip it in the bud before my softhearted alpha made promises I couldn't allow him to keep. "Only during thunderstorms or other random acts of nature. Learn my rule, or I'll have it tattooed on your forehead. Now go to sleep before I get grumpy."

"Too late," Saul observed in a dry tone.

When Matt snorted and said it was about time he found something which made me grouchy, I couldn't quite get mad. Not when I had been celebrating the same exact thing not all that long ago. *Touché*, I thought to myself and decided my puppy pile could figure themselves out. My eyelids were too heavy to fight sleep for another second.

This time as I drifted off, my pout turned into a smile as both of my brothers cuddled against me, and Matt's big arm pinned the three of us down. My last thought as I passed out completely was how very much I loved my life now.

FIFTEEN

MATT

"Hey there, little wolf. How's your morning going?" I smiled and pushed back from the desk as Elisha slipped into my office, closing the door behind him. When he hesitated by a guest chair, I held my arms wide. "Don't even think about it. I need to hold you. It's been too many hours since I saw you last."

He huffed, shooting me an amused smile, but still came over and sat down on my lap. Wrapping my arms around his stomach, I nuzzled the side of his neck before resting my chin on his shoulder. I felt his contentment as he rested a hand over mine and threaded our fingers together. "Breakfast was two hours ago, my love. You barely had time to miss me."

"Two is too many, and I always have time to miss you. What are the boys up to? Oh, before I forget. Jared said yesterday he vetted a good list of candidates for the nanny job. I pointed him in your direction because I knew you'd want to be involved. And let's face it—we both know you're the better one to take the lead since I'm getting a handle on having kids. Did he get a chance to talk to you about it?"

After a few days to settle in and adjust to being a family, we were trying to choose a routine. The problem was, balancing our responsibilities to the pack while finding time for supervising the boys' activities was a lot. It also brought my attention to other things missing in our community, but I hadn't found time to address them yet.

Groaning, Elisha rested his head against mine, seeking comfort. "Never again. Jared told you he had a list? No. Jared had a line of people for me to interview. He sprang them on me while I was going over menus with Paula. It's okay, though. He got in trouble with his mother for stressing me out."

"I don't understand. Why would Jared jump you? I can't believe he didn't put it on your calendar."

"Mr. Efficiency? I doubt he even considered I might want time to get a list of questions together and decide what I was looking for. We barely talked about the idea of hiring a nanny yesterday. Yesterday! And today he had people ready to be interviewed? You'd think it was his personal mission."

Wincing, I realized precisely why Jared might believe it was. "I'm sorry, the conflict is probably my fault. When you were having lunch with Christina yesterday, I had Jared watch the boys while I met with the group of local business owners to discuss the new tax system the Gamma Council voted on. They were happy with the hefty reduction, but when I came out of the meeting, I found Jared cutting gum out of Noah's hair while Saul told him what he was doing wrong."

Elisha shook as he started laughing. "Paula told me. Apparently, the gum came right after a paint incident which didn't go as planned. I meant to ask Saul about it, but he's been hanging out with Devon all morning. Devon made the mistake of walking in with a copy of one of my brother's

THE RELUCTANT ALPHA

favorite books in his back pocket. Apparently, there's a library around here somewhere? Anyway, they went for a visit."

"Yeah, it's in the next town over. Nice of Devon to get him out of the house. As for the paint incident? Here's what you need to know. Jared thought painting would be a good activity. He didn't realize Noah needed hands-on supervision. It's why you didn't see him at dinner last night. He spent hours scrubbing the dining room in his mom's living quarters. Rumor has it Noah got more paint on the furniture than on the paper."

"Oh, God. Poor man! So he wasn't being a jerk—he really was desperate for us to find childcare. Especially with the new baby on the way. Yeah, I get it now. I'm glad I was nice because I'd feel awful if I'd been rude to him."

I gave his fingers a gentle squeeze. "I think we got sidetracked. Tell me about the nannies—did any of them seem like a good candidate?"

He sat up and tried to turn. It only took me a few seconds to have him sitting sideways, where he could see my face. Elisha rolled his eyes. "It's not fair how easy you make moving me seem. I keep getting bigger every day, and it's so much work to make my body do what I want. And then you lift me around like it's nothing. If I didn't like those muscles of yours so much, I might have to hate you." He stopped to run an appreciative hand over my chest.

As much as I enjoyed his touch, I caught his hand and shook my head. "No distractions, little wolf. At least not with the door unlocked. You were about to tell me about the nannies you interviewed, I believe?"

"The nannies. Yes! They were all good, but I found one I want to hire. She's doing a trial run right now and spending time with Noah. Her name is Brenda, and she's overqualified for the position, to be honest. She's in her mid-twenties and has a teaching degree. I didn't meet her before because she was finishing school. Brenda wasn't sure if she was going to come back to the pack or live among the humans, but when her parents told her about us and all the changes we're making, she decided to head home. Which leads me to the next thing I want to talk to you about."

I banged the back of my head against my chair a few times. "Why do I think this is going to cost money? Don't get me wrong—I don't mind. But if I have to sit across the table from Fredo's calculator while the Gamma Council makes me sit through another budget meeting, fair warning, I'm dragging you in there with me." Now that I'd reinstated the powers they should've had within the pack, the gammas had been having a field day. Every time I turned around, another budget meeting or necessary vote had to happen immediately.

Gripping my chin in one hand, Elisha squished my cheeks between his thumb and forefinger to give me fish lips while playfully making my head turn from side to side. "My poor Alpha. He came to save us all, only to suffer a slow death by committee." He squealed and jerked his hand away when I licked his thumb.

Laughing, I booped his nose. "You tease, but I'm most likely to die in the middle of a meeting. But don't worry. They'll have a vote on it first." After shuddering dramatically, I reminded myself we were attempting to have a serious discussion. "Sorry, there was something else you wanted to talk about? First, tell me if you hired the overqualified but seemingly perfect Brenda."

He hummed as he rocked his hands from side to side. "Kinda? I mean, I hired her for now, but I have bigger plans. Do you know what this pack is missing? A school. We have a one-room schoolhouse, but it hasn't been used in several years, from what I was told. After the last teacher left, they couldn't get Horace to hire anyone else. A few families drive their kids to human schools in some of the nearby towns, but it's a hardship, and a few families homeschool, but parents should have a choice. Some of the Newberry Springs people who came here are also qualified teachers. Christina, for one. But I could list a handful of others. And who knows about the pack members I haven't gotten to know yet? Horace didn't let me leave the house very much, so I have a lot to learn about our packmates."

Thinking his words over, I pursed my lips. How had he read my mind? One of the things I'd been considering was how we needed to grow as a pack and offer more things to our community. Most importantly, educational opportunities.

When I said as much to Elisha, he smiled indulgently. "Let me think, could it be because we're on the same page? I'm simply glad I can help. You've had a lot on your plate, and you're still getting a handle on your new job. Even if your dad did prepare you, that was years ago, and I'm sure he hadn't covered a lot because you were young. You're a brand-new pack Alpha, and you're having to rebuild the pack after years of neglect. We're going to come across a lot of things we need around here, and we'll deal with them as they pop up. Don't forget, you've got me at your side. We're a team, right? We both have different strengths we can use to support each other."

"How are you only nineteen? I may have a decade on you and a lot more life experience, but I swear, sometimes, it feels like you're the single grownup in the room. When I was your age, I was sneaking into bars and trying to find myself."

No doubt about it, Elisha was unusually mature for his age. I knew a lot of it came from how he grew up. But my grandmother would've said he was an old soul. I'd never given much thought to the old expression, but it fit Elisha. Maybe there was more truth than folksy wisdom in my grandma's old sayings.

Cheeks pink, Elisha smiled shyly at the praise. "Thank you. It means a lot to hear you say so. It's hard being an authority figure when I'm often the youngest person in the room. I'd also like to point out that I was raised for this, too. Like your dad knew you would be his heir, mine had always planned I would be First Mate with the Alpha of his choosing."

He rolled his eyes at the memory of his father's plans for him. "And while Dad insisted I was trained so I wouldn't embarrass him, my papa wanted me to be able to confidently run my home. I was younger than Noah when he started. Our tea parties included napkin folding and proper silverware placement." He paused for a moment, smiling wistfully at the memory.

I loved hearing him talk. He always had so much to say, and all of it was important and interesting. Elisha gave his head a shake and got back to business. "But enough reminiscing. What do you think about getting the school going again? You realize this is also a problem for us personally, right? We either have to hire a tutor or send them to school. Whatever we choose, we should do it sooner than later. It's summer, but the new school year will be starting soon, and we need to have something lined up for them."

"Shit. You're not wrong. We have to get something figured out and fast. Hard decision, though. On the one hand, I think mixing with the pack and getting socialization would be good for the boys. Human kids need it too, but wolf pups thrive on it. I would've been lost if I hadn't been able to go to school. But we also have to think about their security. I don't want to be like your dad and hide them away at home or start tunneling an underground city. I suppose we have deltas to keep them safe, though. They can patrol the school easily enough."

I was mostly thinking out loud, but security was an equally important aspect to consider. Especially since an outsider knew there were young omegas in our pack. "I never should've risked bringing Bart here. Sure, his pack can be a good line of defense if one or more of the city alphas decide to head our way, but I'm not convinced it was worth the fallout."

Resting his head on my shoulder, Elisha rubbed a hand over my chest. "You were doing your best, and finding allies was a good idea. Don't let Bart's disgusting question make you second-guess yourself. We each have our strengths, remember? I like focusing on pack needs, like educating our young, beautifying the community, and making sure everyone's happy and well fed."

He paused to kiss the underside of my chin. "But Matt? Safety is paramount, and the sole reason I'm free to relax enough to handle my jobs is because you made me feel secure. You've made the choices you have so far for safety. Besides, it's not your fault those stupid city alphas want to chase you down because they think you're some young punk who won't see them coming. If they do attack, it'll be because they've underestimated you. And finding allies, whether you like them or not, is further proof you're on top of our security needs."

"You're so good for me. I don't know how I ever existed without you, little wolf. I didn't realize how big a job I was taking on with this pack, but I don't regret it for a second.

Not only because I feel this is where I'm supposed to be in my bones, but getting to be your mate is worth whatever I have to do. And I don't have any doubts we're building a strong pack and a good community here."

Elisha lifted his head to give me a soft, sweet kiss. After he pulled away, he sat up straight. "I might have a solution. Since the schoolhouse is going to need repairs after sitting so long—I know as much without checking the place out—what if we held school here in the community room? I'll need to get to work on this right away. But I'm willing to take the lead on the project if it's okay with you. I can meet with Christina and Brenda and whatever other educationally minded people we have in the pack. Get some suggestions, run a few ideas around, and then I can touch base with you before I proceed. Although I would need a budget."

Groaning, I rolled my head back to stare at the ceiling. "And now we're back to money." I was chuckling as I looked back at him. "Remember, you have to attend whatever budget meetings the Gamma Council requires for it, but yes. Please feel free to make this your pet project and run with it. All I need is a promise you won't hesitate to ask for help if you need anything." Resting my hand on his belly, I rubbed a gentle circle while I held his gaze. "And don't overdo it. Take a lesson from Paula and learn to delegate. She wears herself out because she has to oversee everything."

"I'm a step ahead of you, Matt. I've been doing a lot less since the boys arrived, anyway. I wanted to spend time with them and reconnect. And I know once the baby comes, I'll want bonding time. My plan is to get people on board who know what they're doing and let them handle it. I'll stay on top of everything, but our family will always take priority."

"You know what you need? A Jared." I held up a hand at his startled laugh. "I don't mean another beta—Jared would never allow it anyway. But in addition to everything he does to keep track of the pack, he's a valuable assistant, and I'd be lost without him. Yes, this is exactly what you need, and I'm going to see about getting you some help. Hell, how about I mention it to Jared and let him make it happen?"

Elisha hesitated before smiling as the idea grew more appealing. "You don't think I'm too young? Because I can think of a lot of things an assistant could do for me to make life a lot easier."

"Age is nothing but a number, or so they say, and has nothing to do with your workload or need for help. You're doing so many things around here, and you've proven yourself more responsible than half the adults I've come across. So... are you saying yes?"

He grinned with a mischievous look in his eye. "Yes, but let's have Jared do the interviewing. He knows what I'm looking for." I chuckled at his subtle payback for the nanny fiasco. The funniest thing was I knew Jared would love handling it.

Right on cue, a tap sounded on my door, and Jared poked his head in. "Sorry to interrupt, but I have an interesting situation requiring your attention."

Elisha lowered his leg as if ready to get up. "Did you need both of us, or should I give you privacy?"

Stepping in and closing the door, Jared looked as excited as Noah on pancake day. "No, please stay. The deltas called me to the main checkpoint when a guy showed up in a big moving truck with a small caravan of cars behind him."

Okay, my interest was piqued. "I take it there wasn't anything to be concerned about?"

"Not at all. When I got there, I met a man named Diego Rodriguez. He's a strong wolf and educated. The rest of the party includes his mate and their pups, along with his mate's parents and siblings. Altogether, two families with a total of nine people are petitioning to join our pack."

Pausing, Jared looked directly at Elisha. "You might know them. The mate grew up in Newberry Springs. She moved after meeting Diego in college. Her name was Isabel Rosen."

"Isabel's a good wolf, from what I recall. Her whole family left the pack when she did. Her sisters are my age. Their family wasn't happy after my papa died, and there was nobody to intervene when Dad got out of control. The last I heard, they'd moved to San Diego."

Jared bobbed his head in agreement. "She told me the exact same thing. The family was in the process of moving back east where Diego was offered a job. Diego heard about all the changes here through the grapevine, and when he talked to Isabel about it, she urged him to stop here on the way. If we don't accept them, they'll head on out to Oklahoma."

I wasn't understanding his excitement, beyond growing our pack. "If we have housing, I say go for it. As pack beta, you have the authority to bring new pack members in if they meet with your approval. Do you want me to come meet them now and officially add them after they bend the knee?"

He'd been hovering near the door, but he finally came closer and sat down. "I've already approved them and invited them to dinner tonight for you to accept and add them to the pack. But I haven't told you the best part! Diego is a doctor. He's a general practitioner licensed to practice in this state, and there's more!"

THE RELUCTANT ALPHA

My hand automatically went back to Elisha's belly. "What's the best part?"

Rubbing his hands together, Jared looked downright gleeful. "Diego ran his own clinic with Isabel as his nurse and office manager. Plus, he has all his equipment on the back of his truck. He's prepared to set up a clinic without any delays. As soon as tomorrow, we could have our own doctor. Isaac isn't going to be thrilled—he thinks the only healer necessary is an epsilon. But I disagree. Our human sides often need human medicine."

I snorted at the mention of Isaac. "Do you know I haven't met him yet? He took off the day I got here on his spirit quest or whatever you said it was. He might not even be coming back. And we have a baby on the way, so it goes without saying—I'm in favor of having a doctor around."

"Close, it's a moon quest." No matter what his personal thoughts might have been on the man himself, Jared radiated complete respect while talking about Isaac's spirituality. "You'll meet him after the new moon. Once a year, Isaac goes deep into the desert. I don't know what all he does out there, but he always comes back with predictions for the pack. He does something similar at winter solstice, but he stays close."

"As fascinating as the idea is—and I can't wait to meet the man—I'm still in favor of Dr. Diego. Now, unless we have more pack business to cover, I suggest we head to the dining room. My stomach says it's lunchtime."

At lunch, I got to meet Brenda, and I was impressed by how well she was already connecting with Noah. My young mate had no reason to second-guess himself. He'd chosen well for our nanny, even if she was overqualified. She and Elisha talked about educational ideas she had for both boys to keep their brains engaged until school started, as well as fun activities too. We'd probably need someone else for the baby, but it was good to know our older boys would be in capable hands.

The rest of the afternoon was spent in yet another budget meeting. Finally, I got to break away to check in with the newly appointed Delta leaders and watch them run the men through an obstacle course. Things were definitely looking up in this pack. It was early days yet, but I could already see a bright future.

After dinner, Elisha introduced me to Isabel and her family. Once each adult bent the knee and extended their wrist for my bite, I was thrilled to add them to our numbers. More impressive, they'd spent the afternoon getting moved into their new pack-assigned housing. Adding new members with specialized skills was always good, but discovering they were hard workers who wouldn't shy away from work was a bonus.

True to his word, Diego already had his clinic set up the following day. Right at the end of the street, the new clinic operated in an empty storefront, formerly a deli when I was growing up. Naturally, I made sure Elisha was the first patient after learning one of his pieces of equipment was an ultrasound machine.

His mind was on so many things, Elisha had grumbled about making room in his schedule for this visit. He wasn't being too obvious, but I could sense it through our bond. And the frequent glimpses at his phone to check the time. I didn't mind because I always thought this rarely viewed side of him was adorable. If he knew how cute I thought he was when he got grouchy, he probably wouldn't be amused.

"Smile, little wolf. You're going to like this next part, I promise. I saw an ultrasound once, when my grandpa had kidney stones. It was pretty cool, but somehow I think this is going to be a lot better."

Elisha lifted a brow. "I've never seen an ultrasound, and I've also never visited a human doctor. Dad only had use for epsilon healers. But if we're going to see the baby, I certainly *hope* it will be a lot better than kidney stones." He kicked his feet and wiggled impatiently on the table. "I don't see why Isabel made me pee in a cup or wear this ridiculous gown. How invasive is this test? Surely Dr. Diego could've just lifted my shirt, right?"

The door opened at the perfect moment for Dr. Diego and Isabel to walk in. Laughing, she wagged a finger at Elisha. "The gown is necessary because the doctor needs to do an initial exam. The urine test was to check a few things to make sure you and the pup are both healthy. Now quit pouting and lie back, put your feet in the stirrups, and go to your happy place while my mate examines you. Don't worry. It won't hurt."

Elisha was definitely pouting. "You said the same thing about the blood pressure test. You didn't tell me you would squeeze the life out of my arm." The two of them bickered playfully. Isabel did her best to distract him while Dr. Diego quickly got through the embarrassing portion of the physical examination. When he dribbled goo on Elisha's stomach to run the wand over it, my grumpy little wolf squirmed unhappily.

Until Isabel hit a switch, and a loud whooshing sound accompanied by a rapid heartbeat filled the air. Elisha's eyes widened with wonder as Isabel explained we were hearing the baby's heartbeat. His smile only grew when he looked on the screen and saw our son.

"Congratulations, gentlemen. You're having a boy." Dr. Diego's cheerful statement had Elisha squeezing my hand with barely contained glee. I didn't bother to hold it in, doctor's office or not. I bent to kiss my mate, holding him close for a few moments.

A son. We were having another boy join our family.

Dr. Diego was happy to take his time, letting us enjoy the moment before getting back to the exam. He took a few measurements before turning to Elisha, peering at him over the top of his reading glasses. "All right, young man. You and the pup are both in good shape. From the dates you gave me, your son is exactly where we want him to be in the beginning of the third month. For the next six weeks or so, he's going to grow at a more rapid pace. Isabel will give you a list of things to watch out for, and I want you to call me day or night if you have cause for alarm."

I liked his calm, quiet manner. But I was even more of a fan of the kind aura he projected. Dr. Diego continued to chat, setting Elisha at ease in the process. "A nine-month pregnancy is hard for a human woman and worse for female shifters, who do it in six. But their experience is nothing compared to what the omega body gets put through in their short four months of gestation."

As if the thought of a four-month pregnancy was too much for her to contemplate, Isabel shivered. "Listen to the doctor, Eli. Staying active is good for you. But don't be afraid to rest, too. Take as many naps as you want. Your body knows what it needs, so listen to it." She and her husband definitely made a good team, and our pack was lucky to have them.

All conversation came to a halt when Dr. Diego put a printout of a sonogram image in Elisha's hands. When we got home, my sweet little wolf was still smiling.

SIXTEEN

ELISHA

AFTER A WHOLE MONTH went by without so much as a whisper of danger, we decided it was safe to have a big party. I turned down more than one offer to throw me a baby shower, so I was hoping today would give everyone the opportunity they needed to congratulate us and offer their best wishes.

Honestly, I was just happy to get together as a community. We had so much to celebrate. Our entire town looked better than ever. Buildings had been painted, overgrown grass and weeds cut back, windows replaced and potholes filled. Main Street had a whole new vibe—less ghost town and more small-town Americana.

And even better? Two separate community gardens had been planted. If the special fertilizer I provided was so good the seeds were already sprouting, nobody questioned it.

Thankfully, the weather forecast had been right on the money. We were having a rare cool day—meaning it was a paltry hundred and five in the shade—and everything was all set up for our barbecue. A row of grills were set up in front of the diner, and the sidewalk was lined with tables, filled with all the dishes and desserts people brought for the potluck.

Hank, a regular wolf shifter who owned the diner, oversaw the grilling area. The Gamma Council provided the meat, and Hank insisted on making sure it was properly cooked. Since he was originally from Texas, I figured he was probably the perfect man for the job. Tables and chairs had been set up in the middle of the street for the occasion. It was completely safe because the street was closed off in either direction.

Our pack was over three hundred strong, and I was still getting to know people. Matt and I had spent the past hour wandering through the street, meeting and greeting our neighbors but mostly letting them see us happily involved. After I was done mingling—at least, my feet were—I didn't even argue when Matt lifted me and carried me back to our own table.

Nuzzling his neck, I kissed the pulse point where his scent ran strong. "My feet want to thank your big muscles for the ride. I don't think I can eat another bite, but I wouldn't hate it if you found me another glass of lavender lemonade."

After depositing me on my chair, Matt gave me a quick kiss before straightening. "One lemonade, coming up. Do you boys need anything?" Saul and Noah looked up from the huge dessert plates they were crouched over like a pair of feral cats. Saul looked guilty when he saw me, but Noah shook his chocolate-covered face at Matt. Snorting, I waved him off. "These little pigs are fine. But if you see any more of those hand wipes, we could definitely use them."

Lucian looked up from his equally full dessert plate. "I had a plan, Eli." Yes, Matt's buddies had taken to calling me by my childhood nickname after hearing my brothers use it too many times. I didn't mind. I actually liked it. It made me feel like part of their group. Matt waited, obviously interested. Knowing Lucian, I wasn't entirely sure I wanted to know.

I lifted a brow and motioned for him to continue. "A plan, huh? I can't wait to hear this one."

Grinning now, Lucian pointed at the fire hydrant across the street. "Look at the kid—he's got so much sugar on him an army of bees would be scared to take on the job. He needs a good pressure washing. I figure we can hook a hose up and blast him with it."

Before I could close my mouth long enough to formulate a reply, two of our largest delta wolves came running toward us. Their huge, furry gray bodies slipped through the tables as gracefully as ballerinas. Barely coming to a stop, they shifted to human form. The guys were already rising, on full alert and ready to assist with whatever.

Matt's voice was deceptively calm, though I could feel the coiled tension he was doing his best to hide from the boys. "What's going on? Walk with me. There's no need to discuss this in front of the family." As he led them away, Lucian and the guys stayed close to watch over us.

They didn't get far enough because I clearly heard one of the deltas speak. "It was the exact same white Escalade. The guy who came here for lunch last month? He showed up with three other alphas. We turned them away at the checkpoint. I told him the road was closed for a pack potluck. He wanted me to call you to the gate, but I told him he would need to call you and make an appointment. He said something about being an ally and how I would get in trouble for this, but I was firm. I explained my instructions were to turn away outsiders today."

"I see." Matt's voice was icy. I could feel his indignation

and wished I was close enough to offer a comforting touch. "I take it they didn't leave peacefully?"

"No, Alpha. He backed up and started to turn as if he was going to leave. But he swerved around the barrier and went off the road through the desert. A bunch of us deltas are tracking them, but we can't keep up with a vehicle. And he can take whatever route he wants with four-wheel drive."

My entire body froze, and I definitely peed a little as the white Escalade in question barreled between two buildings, driving straight at us. Before any of us had a chance to react, the SUV came to a stop, and the driver's door swung open.

Matt stiffened. "I want you two deltas to guard my family. Stay in wolf form and protect them with your lives." A wave of affection and encouragement shot through our bond as Matt glanced over his shoulder. Flashing me a wink, he motioned for Lucian, Tucker, and Devon. "Can you guys give me a hand? I need to take care of something over here. Brace yourselves, everyone."

Dozens of deltas in wolf form swarmed from every direction, surrounding the crowd and putting themselves between the pack and the source of danger. As those other two deltas shifted back into wolf form, Saul scooted closer to me while Noah slipped under the table. Before I had a chance to panic, he popped up between us and burrowed himself against my side. One of the deltas actually jumped onto the table, crouching in front of us and snarling toward the intruders. The other stood at my side, pressing up against me as if already trying to become a shield as Matt had instructed.

Even as I clocked all these details, my eyes never left the scene playing out in front of me. An arrogant-looking blond man, presumably Bart, got out on the driver's side, quickly joined by the other men. Like every other alpha-hole on the planet, they sent a wave of power out to let everyone know how big and bad they were. When all three immediately shifted without taking time to undress, any slight hope I might have had that they meant no harm was blown away, much like the clothes shredded during their shift.

Matt and the guys all shifted and took off at a run, the tattered remains of their own clothing dropping to the street behind them. When our bond went blank, alarm shot through me, making every hair on my body stand on end. I wanted to scream and pound my fist against the table while I shouted every bad word I could think of. But I remembered what he'd said about blocking the pack consciousness to avoid distractions.

Since our bond flowed both ways, maybe he was protecting both of us? If that was the case, I definitely wanted my man to focus without anyone's emotions disrupting him. Even if those emotions were mine.

I'm not sure what I expected, but this wasn't the polite, regulated fight circle, and nobody was following any rules. Matt was easy to keep track of: he was the sole silver-and-black wolf out there. Lucian's wolf was snow white, so he was also obvious. The other wolves were a mix of gray and brown. If I were closer, or if they'd stop moving long enough, I could probably pick out Tucker's dark muzzle or Devon's caramel-colored paws.

From here, though? It was like watching a dogfight. Fangs gleamed, and claws struck, but mostly it was a swirling pile of fur. My heart pounded painfully against my rib cage as Matt and Lucian fended off attack after attack while dealing their own blows in return. Hugging Noah tightly, I kept his face pressed against my chest so he couldn't see the nightmare unfolding in front of us. I didn't have to worry about Saul, thanks to the wall of deltas blocking his view.

When I thought I couldn't handle another second, it was over, almost as fast as it began. Two gray wolves fell to the street in the telltale shift between human and wolf which only came after another alpha's killing bite. Medeina poison was no joke. Another wolf went down, also a victim of an alpha's laniary teeth.

Matt was still fighting, and I could barely handle watching, so I looked for the other guys. Since I didn't know yet who'd fallen, I was relieved to immediately recognize the other three standing. Tucker and Devon joined Lucian to circle around the two fighting wolves, ready to jump in and help Matt if necessary.

It wasn't. The brown wolf jumped up at Matt. Matt caught him midair and bit into the wolf's stomach, jerking his head. Taking a long roping piece of intestine with him, he eviscerated the other wolf. After the brown wolf fell, Matt went in for another strike. The dying wolf had enough blood pumping through him to change forms. When they finally stopped shifting, I was glad three of them remained in fur form. The one Lucian had taken out reverted to human—the arrogant blond man who had brought them here.

A wave of protectiveness and love swept through our now-open bond. His attention only on me, Matt left the bodies where they'd fallen. The other guys stayed by the SUV, keeping watch over the remains until something could be done. I kissed the top of Noah's head and whispered softly, "We're safe now. Matt and the guys took care of everything." I gently guided him to Saul and struggled to my feet. The delta protecting me barely had time to get out of the way before Matt was at my side, helping me the rest of the way up and pulling me into his arms. So relieved everything was okay now, I burst into tears.

When I was able to speak, I thumped a fist against his shoulder. "Either quit blocking me or teach me to do it. I have to remember to make you tell me your trick."

His strong hand gripped my chin and tilted my face back so he could smother my mouth with hungry, possessive kisses. I didn't care about standing in the middle of the pack potluck with my naked, filth-covered alpha kissing the heck out of me right in front of my brothers. Matt and everyone else I loved was safe. Once again, my alpha had saved us all.

Matt broke the kiss almost reluctantly, barely pulling away enough to rub his nose against mine as he pressed our foreheads together. When he spoke, processing what he was saying took several seconds. "Reach for our bond like the living thing it is. Make a picture in your mind to represent it. I use a ribbon of water for mine. Then imagine a brick wall stopping its flow."

I immediately tried it, and it worked. Matt barely had time to react before I imagined the brick wall blowing to smithereens. He leaned his head back with a questioning look. "You had it. I see your point now because I didn't like it, but why did you drop the wall so fast?"

"Because I was lonely on the other side. I don't like not being able to sense you, even if the block is under my own control." Looking like he wanted to melt, he jerked me into another deep kiss. He finally let me go so he could make sure the boys were okay.

Matt held a hand out to give Noah a high-five. "Thanks for keeping an eye on your brothers while I took out the trash. I knew I could count on you, little man. How about I save our hugs for later after I'm showered and dressed?" When Noah giggled, Matt smiled and turned his concerned gaze to Saul. "What about you, big man? Everything okay, or do you want to hug it out?"

Matt's little bit of levity was all Saul needed. His tight expression of fear and worry relaxed into an eye roll and a smirk. "No thanks. I'll pass on hugging the dirty naked dude. Talk to me after you've showered. Hopefully with bleach. You should probably use a whole tube of toothpaste while you're at it. I hate to break it to you, but you got some stanky breath going on. Eli must really love you if he kissed your mouth right now."

I closed my eyes and looked up at the sky, letting the sunlight wash over me and fill me with peace. When Jared spoke, I opened them again.

"Good job out there, Alpha. I took the liberty of contacting the territory chief. As it happens, he was having lunch with the Riverside Alpha. He's on his way now. He promised it wouldn't be long."

While I sat back down and pulled up a chair to rest my feet on, Matt released the deltas and took a few minutes to reassure the pack. Brenda made my day, setting a glass of lemonade and a big fudge brownie in front of me. I looked her in the eye and spoke straight from the heart. "I hate to break it to you, but I think I'm in love with you now. If I wasn't already mated, I would do something awkward like hug you."

She laughed and gave me a quick squeeze. "Hugs are never awkward, Eli. I figured you could use some sugar before the adrenaline crash, which I'm sure isn't far behind. Listen, I know it's supposed to be my day off, but you need me more than I need a break. I doubt I'll be able to pull you away from the Alpha's side anytime soon. But how about I take these two home? The party's breaking up anyway, and I think we can agree Noah could use a bath."

Noah. Bath. Right, he was covered in chocolate. Groaning, I glanced down at my shirt and saw a big chocolate smear where I'd held his sticky little face against me. I allowed myself an eight-second pity party before shaking it off. Messy kids were a fact of life. I looked at his dirty face and wrinkled my nose. "Brenda's on the money, short stuff. You need a bath. What do you think, would you like to go home with Brenda? Matt and I have some boring stuff to handle, and we're going to be here talking to adults for a while."

While Noah pursed his lips and looked longingly at my brownie, Saul was already on his feet, obviously done with today. Leaning over Noah, he gave me a quick hug before skirting around to join Brenda. "I'm gonna go with, in case Brenda needs a hand." A flash of his future adult self appeared as he looked at Noah with a stern expression. "Leave Eli's brownie alone. He's eating for two, and our nephew needs the chocolate more than you do. Come on. It's rude to keep Brenda waiting."

Managing to keep a straight face, I thanked Brenda for her help. Thankfully, I enjoyed my treat and downed the liquid refreshment before Ash pulled up beside the now-abandoned Escalade. This time, I walked hand in hand with Matt as he went to deal with our new guest. At least this one was invited. Efficient as ever, Jared found a pair of jogging pants for Matt and three more for the other guys, so at least he wasn't naked as he greeted Ash.

Ash took one look at the dead wolves and the SUV before shaking his head in disgust. As he came forward to shake our hands, he blew out a breath and shoved his sunglasses to the top of his head. "Good afternoon, gentlemen. I swear, Matt. You must have a target on your back or something. I haven't seen this much activity around here in years." He motioned toward the dead wolves. "I'm sorry as hell, Matt. You were well within your rights to defend yourself, so there won't be any official investigation necessary. Especially with an outright act of war, considering Alpha Macklebee is officially registered as an ally to your pack."

"Yeah, I figured as much. Thank you for confirming it, though. Do you know who these other households were?" While Matt spoke, the other guys shifted back and slipped into the pants Jared offered them before walking over to join the conversation.

Nodding, Ash pointed at Bart. "Let's go one at a time. First, did you personally deliver the killing bite to each of these men? I only ask because I need to know who is taking over their packs."

At the horrified look on Lucian's face, I would've laughed. The unclaimed alpha who thought nobody wanted him was getting a pack of his own. And a rich one, from what I'd heard. Smiling sympathetically, Matt motioned to Lucian. "Ash, I'd like to introduce you to Lucian Smith. I think we both know I couldn't have taken out four alphas on my own, no matter what the legends swirling around the territory have to say about me. You have Lucian to thank for relieving the world of Bart Macklebee the Third."

Ash took one look at Lucian's unmarked chest and whistled as if impressed. "Well, I guess we can all agree you never expected to be in this position. Good for you. Any friend of Matt's is a man I'm willing to trust. I don't care where you came from—I just want to know if you can handle a pack. What do you say, are you willing to accept what's rightfully yours according to our governing laws?"

Lucian considered it before nodding at Ash with a cocky grin. "What the hell. It'll be fun to put those rich fucks in their place. Hopefully, they won't all be assholes."

"No, you'll find a lot of decent, hard-working people over there. And the ones who aren't can either fall into place or petition for a new placement." Ash grinned unrepentantly. "And here's where I get to have fun. Let me know if they fuck with you. I'll put them somewhere in the Central Valley where the cow shit hangs so strong in the air you can taste it."

As Ash moved on to the other wolves, he recognized them but confirmed their markings with pictures he had on file in his phone, alongside their human likeness and pack information. The next one was Devon's kill, hailing from a small town named Hemet. Ash went through the same routine, asking if Devon was willing to accept what was rightfully his to take.

Devon held his hands out, motioning toward his friends. "Since heading up packs seems to be what the West Coast Wolves are doing nowadays, it seems fair I step up. What kind of pack am I getting? Because I've been through Hemet, and it's a one-horse town if I've ever seen one."

Ash chuckled his agreement. "The best description I've ever heard. Let's see, it says here it's a small pack with a few dozen members. They have a different setup. The pack owns about fifty acres on the outside of town and lives commune-style in a single pack house. They blend in with humans because of the whole hippie look. They're also farmers, but it's not grapes they're growing. In addition to the vegetables they sell at the local farmer's market, they have a crop of medicinal-grade marijuana they grow for a local dispensary."

Lucian got a kick out of the idea. "Score. After all these years, the West Coast Wolves can finally meet the biker stereotype. Too bad we're all gonna be too busy being responsible to ride the roads and rub it in everyone's faces.

Seriously, though, I end up with the wine pack, and Devon inherited a pot farm. The only thing missing is for one of these guys to get a secret whorehouse operation."

"Sorry, I'm afraid not. Although this alpha over there was from one of the property-less LA packs. And when I say small, I mean it. There's about fifteen of them, and they've been renting a group of homes in a cul-de-sac down in Westwood for a few years now. I believe the pack consists of three families and a handful of single guys who operate as the deltas. The good news is you didn't make any enemies because he didn't have a mate or any family. Same goes for all of them, by the way. Probably should've mentioned it. I imagine they joined forces because of it." Ash hesitated before looking back at Matt.

"I'm not sure if you know, but when your beta called, I was having lunch with the Riverside Alpha. He's an old friend, and he cautioned me to warn you when I told him about what happened. Apparently, one of his reasons for wanting to meet with me was so you'd know word was traveling around about the two young omegas in your care." When Matt immediately took up a defensive posture, Ash held up a hand. "Don't worry. I already knew about Monty's boys. I had my office send gifts when they were born, in fact. While I had no use for Monty, his mate was a childhood friend. Steve and I weren't close after his father mated him to Monty—it simply wasn't possible. But I kept tabs on him as much as I could."

Matt relaxed slightly, but his voice still had a growly undertone. "Then you know how sickening it is for four grown-ass alphas to attack my pack so they could take it over and get control of two little boys. You might want to spread the news—I've replaced Monty's X with my own. They aren't just in my care. They're my family, and I'll protect them against anything waiting to hurt them."

"Fair enough, and nothing less than I expected. Now let's get this over with because it's damned hot here, and the bodies are starting to stink." Ash was mostly joking, but we really did need to get these bodies gone sooner than later. Sighing, Ash pointed at the final wolf. "That's one of your neighbors. I was surprised when I didn't see an alliance agreement cross my desk with his name on it. He led the Barstow pack butting right up to your territory. They have about seventy-five members, if I recall. I'll have to check the file to make sure. First, which one of you was responsible for him?"

Matt held up a hand. "Interestingly enough, me. I guess my territory expanded, now didn't it?"

"Sounds like it. I take it you won't be giving his pack away, huh?" Ash teased, checking his phone before looking up again. "I was close. Seventy-seven members. I'll note you're accepting what's rightfully yours."

"No point leaving them leaderless, not when they're close enough to absorb into my pack. I'll file whatever paperwork is necessary to merge the packs into one."

Scratching the side of his neck, Ash looked around at the different alphas. "Sounds good. Have your beta contact my office. They'll tell him what to do. What about the Alpha from Westwood? Since we have another alpha standing here, I'm gonna go out on a limb and say he was your handiwork?" His eyes settled on Tucker, who immediately nodded. Ash winced. "I hate to say it, but you'll face the same problem he did—lack of space among the humans, with limited opportunities for pack runs."

Tucker took that in, looking down at the dead wolf before squaring his jaw as he looked back up. "You'd be correct in that he was my kill. What happens if I don't want the pack? Or if I took them on, do you think you're attached to where they are? I don't want to leave them defenseless, but I'm not a big fan of the LA basin. You said they rent, right? Maybe your office could help me find some land to buy within the territory, providing the pack has any money to speak of."

"There's the rub. I can offer them places up north with space, but they don't have any money. They touch base every six months, hoping to find abandoned or foreclosed pack lands they can pick up for a song. It happens sometimes when packs lose their way, but it's not as common out here as it is in other territories. If you don't take them, I imagine they will probably disband and become part of other packs. Might be the best thing all around, considering."

When Ash was done, Matt spoke up, turning to Tucker with an excited gleam in his eye. "What if I could offer you some land? I'd have to run it by the Gamma Council, but I don't see why they'd have a problem. Especially when we've now gained Barstow. I'd be willing to sublet a corner of our territory to your pack. I know precisely the spot, too—Apple Valley. You know the area because we had to pass right through it on the way to the neutral spot for the challenge last month. We aren't doing anything with the land. It's sitting there, unused. And given its location, with enough time and some old-fashioned ingenuity, you could probably build something and eventually buy the land if you wanted. But don't think you can ever talk me out of Barstow. Won't happen."

"Why not? Do you have a driving need to control the area surrounding the only highway to Vegas?" Tucker grinned, then looked down as he considered the offer. "You know what? I like it. Not only will it give the city wolves a way out of their urban hell, but it keeps all of us within shouting distance." He nodded to Ash. "I'll do it. I officially accept what's rightfully mine."

"Sounds good." Ash took a moment to shake each of their hands, saving Matt for last. He held on to Matt's hand longer than the others. "I have to tell you, Matt. I like having you around. You make my job easier than it's ever been. Be careful, though. You might get marked to take my place one day."

As if scalded, Matt yanked his hand back. "No thanks, Ash. There's no political aspirations here. I'm a small-town alpha who wants to live a peaceful life with my mate and raise a family within a loyal pack."

SEVENTEEN

MATT

Two weeks to the day after those rat bastards tried to come after me, Elisha went into labor. I woke to find him growling and covered in sweat, sitting in a puddle where his water had broken.

When the contraction making him bite his fist and growl through the pain finally subsided, I stupidly asked why he hadn't gotten me up sooner. His snarled response—I could fuck off because he thought one of us deserved to sleep as long as we could—still made me chuckle when I thought about it.

No one but my always-sweet-but-sometimes-grouchy little wolf could consider my needs while also telling me to fuck off. As much as I wanted to shake him for going through pain alone, I wisely kept my mouth shut and called the doc instead.

He arrived in record time, thank fuck. Elisha was having a lot of pain, but the delivery itself was apparently one of Dr. Diego's faster ones because Elisha was already fully dilated and crowning upon his initial exam.

Dr. Diego turned out to be a true godsend because

Steven's umbilical cord was looped around his neck. Thanks to his quick reaction and years of experience, the doc was able to save him. The idea of my cousin-son—Elisha's favorite thing to call him—not surviving his own birth gave me chills.

From the moment I laid eyes on him, I loved that boy. He'd been shy in the womb and never kicked when I tried to catch him at it. No matter what Elisha did, the little shit wouldn't perform. He'd kick for the boys, for my buddies, hell... he kicked for Jared. But not me.

He'd made up for it since he met me, though. When he was crying, nobody could calm him but Daddy. Elisha could come close, but I was the only one he wanted during the hardcore middle-of-the-night screamfests, where he was dry, fed, and still pissed as hell. I told Elisha it was a Longclaw thing. He might not biologically be my son, but he was blood, and I was his daddy. Anyone who said otherwise could fight me.

Based on his attitude and bloodline, I was pretty sure he was an alpha. Alphas tended to run in my family, to tell the truth. However, if he turned out to be a regular wolf or one of the stronger deltas, I would love and accept him just the same. He didn't have the smaller genitals or telltale dark line along the center of his scrotum marking him as an omega, so we could rule the idea out.

As for the other possibilities, we'd have to wait and see when he was strong enough to shift in a few months. His scent would tell us the answer in shifted form, even as an infant. I smiled down at the baby, nestled in the crook of my arm and staring at me like he wanted to share the secrets of the universe but couldn't since he lacked the power of speech.

"What's on your mind, Stevie? I gotta tell you, I like

these quiet one-on-one times at three in the morning. It's good bonding. But do you know, if you'd sleep like a normal person right now, we could have this same bonding session while also enjoying watching the sunrise? Something to think about, tiny dude."

As Elisha slipped into the room, the nursery light clicked on. "Are you in here pretending to have a conversation with your cousin-son again? I'm starting to think you wake him up somehow so you don't miss this time together."

I snorted, shaking my head at my little wolf. "Elisha, I swear on my mother's grave—you've got to quit calling him that before it becomes a thing. It's funny, especially because it's true, but maybe we could be like normal folks and sweep our circular family tree under the rug?"

He knelt beside the glider, brushing a kiss over the top of Stevie's head before smiling at me. "Okay, I'll stop teasing you. Mostly because I don't need a reminder of Horace. But when I do quit, it might also have something to do with Noah asking me what it meant yesterday. I didn't know what to say, so I gave him a cookie and changed the subject. It's probably best not to remind him."

Elisha reached over my arm to pull the blanket back, unzipping Stevie's jammies just enough to rub his fingertip over the small X over his heart. Eyes filled with devotion, he looked back up at me. "He's your son in every meaningful way anyway, so forget Horace."

"Hey, it's like I said when I sealed the scratch mark after I claimed him. I licked him, so he's mine. Your brothers are my kids too. And whenever you're ready to go again, I'm going to fill your belly with our next pup." When his eyes narrowed, I was quick to backtrack. "Only if you want more. I mean, I'm good with the three boys we already have. But you're young. Hell, so am I. We have plenty of time. You could do it like your papa and space them out six years. Since Stevie is six years younger than Noah, you're already on track."

He watched me struggle through the last part, then laughed. "Wow. I'm... *wow*. Is my big, strong alpha afraid of little ol' me? I must be meaner than I thought when I get grumpy."

"Actually, you're super cute. I didn't want to sound like another toxic alpha who wanted to keep his mate pregnant. I don't need a bunch of pups to show I'm a man. You know what I do need? You. Our family. The rest of the West Coast Wolves. Everything else is gravy. I'm proud of our pack and what we're building here, and I treasure every member. But if it all went away tomorrow, I'd be okay as long as I had us."

Elisha studied me. "The funny thing is, I know you mean every word. As long as you could still provide for us, you really wouldn't care if it all went away. Even though you're arguably one of the best pack Alphas in the territory."

I carefully leaned over Stevie to touch my forehead to his. "I do mean it. I love our pack, don't get me wrong. But I don't need the A in alpha capitalized, if I'm making any sense. In my book, an alpha is a man who keeps his word, takes care of his responsibilities, and uses the strength and power he was given to protect those who need it. Who could possibly need it more than my own family? I get everything I could ever want by looking in your eyes. When you're proud of me, I know I'm living right."

"Then you must feel like the most righteous man alive because I'm always proud of you, my love. Now how about you rock back and forth in the glider and see if you can't get our son to go back to sleep? At the risk of sounding selfish, I'd like a turn being held by those powerful alpha arms."

Holding my other arm out, I nodded toward my lap. "Stevie doesn't take up much space, and neither do you. Also, I'm a big guy with a big lap. Stevie thinks Papa should come cuddle with us, and I agree."

He rolled his eyes but slipped onto my lap and slid one arm around my neck, resting his free hand on Stevie's chest. "Stevie thought so, huh? You must have a telepathic link because I'm pretty sure Stevie didn't say anything. And won't for about a year."

I shook my head sadly at Stevie. "He doesn't mean it, tiny dude. We know you have your own ways of communicating, don't you?"

Elisha gently zipped Stevie's jammies back up and tucked the blanket back in place. "He does, does he? Let me guess, you're the baby whisperer because you know how to translate every cry?"

I snorted. "I wish. No, it's all in his eyes. If you gaze into them long enough, it's like he's talking to you."

"Sweet, my love. But you know what? I think you might need more sleep. The middle-of-the-night sessions are starting to mess with your mind."

We teased each other a little longer until our voices lulled Stevie to sleep more than the glider ever could. Moving so efficiently the baby never stirred, Elisha carefully transferred him to the crib. He turned the lamp off and held out his hand. "Coming, my love? We need to snatch whatever sleep we can get before he wakes us up again."

I grabbed the nursery monitor and rose to take his hand. "Take me to bed, little wolf. Or anywhere else you want. All I know is I'll go wherever you're heading."

"Handy, because I'll never head anywhere without you at my side. Except for the bathroom. Sorry not sorry, but some things are best left private." Love and affection flowed freely through our bond as we walked arm in arm to our bedroom. The moment our heads hit the pillows, Elisha snuggled against me. And I'm dead certain I passed out a few seconds after because his peaceful face was the last thing I remembered before my eyes opened again.

As it happened, Stevie wasn't what woke us a few hours later. My cellphone rang, accompanied by the rumble of a motorcycle pulling into the driveway. I was instantly wide awake. None of my buddies would be coming in hot this early in the morning if something wasn't wrong.

Snatching my phone off the nightstand, I barely had time to register Lucian's name before tapping the screen and putting the phone to my ear as I stepped into my slippers. I was already leaving the room when I said, "Luci. What's up?"

I glanced back when Elisha rushed up behind me. Telling him to stay here was pointless; he wasn't exaggerating when he'd said earlier he would always be at my side. My little wolf meant his words from the bottom of his heart.

"Matty, thank fuck you're awake. Can you let me in the front door? I have a wolf in the sidecar who needs to see your healer." Without giving me a chance to respond, he ended the call—confident in the knowledge I had his back.

He needn't have asked. I ran down the stairs, only to find our mystical epsilon already opening the door. We nodded at each other, and he stepped aside to let me go first. When I got outside, Lucian had already parked and was lifting a small, toffee-colored wolf with matted fur and bloody paws into his arms.

At any other time, I would have joked about Lucian finally finding the perfect furbaby to ride in his sidecar. Except I could tell this wasn't a time for teasing by the amount of pain, fear, and worry I smelled from the two of them. I didn't have to see the way Lucian tenderly cradled the unconscious wolf or sense his possessive vibe to know this wolf was important to my friend.

Once I took a good look and a deeper sniff, I realized his companion was an omega. "Who is this, Luci? Do I need to call the rest of the guys?"

Lucian looked past me to Isaac, standing at the top of the porch and stroking a fist down the length of his long, gray beard. "We can call them later. Right now, I need an epsilon. And yours was the only one I knew of in the area."

Isaac motioned for us to hurry. "Bring him inside. Your young man might not be alert enough to know it, but his body is in a lot of pain."

The older wolf scurried ahead of us. Elisha already had the rarely used elevator open and waiting for us. I followed Lucian inside, making sure everyone was aboard before locking the outer safety gate and closing the doors. Elisha hit the button, and Lucian filled us in while we slowly ascended to the third floor. The elevator might have been convenient at times like this, but its usefulness didn't make the old thing move any faster.

When he caught Elisha's worried gaze on the omega's paws, Lucian explained. "I found him unconscious beside Highway 58, heading back from a moonlight ride. I thought he was an animal at first, since shifters usually revert when we're unconscious. But then I got up close, and I knew as soon as I scented him."

"You knew he was an omega? Or that he's a shifter?" I felt stupid for asking but needed to clarify for absolutely no relevant reason, other than making small talk in the elevator.

Lucian shook his head. "No, neither of those. I knew he

was mine. My true mate. Mine to protect. My responsibility to save. Whatever it takes, I'll do it."

Looking more mystical than a man in corduroy pants and a flannel shirt had a right to, Isaac stroked his beard again. "Don't worry. Thirteen is stuck in this form because his wolf is the sole thing keeping him tethered to our world. Your presence will assist in bringing him back. But first, we must take care of his wounds and alleviate much of the pain. All will be well in the end. It's been foretold."

Looking down at the omega, then back at Isaac, Lucian frowned in confusion. "Why did you call him Thirteen? Do you number your monthly patients or something?"

"Why ever would I do such a thing? No. I called him Thirteen because it is his name. Or rather, the number assigned to this dear, unnamed soul."

Even Elisha did a double take, and he generally rolled with people saying crazy things. "Pardon me for asking, Isaac. But how do you know the details?"

Again with the beard stroking? Isaac rocked back on his heels, managing to look bored as he glanced at my little wolf. "The same way I know everything. My spirit guide told me."

Afterwards, the elevator fell silent because what was left to say? I studied Lucian, pleased to see he had finally found 'the one' but worried at the same time because losing Thirteen before really having him would be a devastating loss, one I wasn't sure Lucian would recover from. My heart broke thinking about it.

A familiar hand slipped into mine, and a comforting wave of love and reassurance flooded our bond. Putting my arm around him, I closed my eyes, holding him against my chest. All I could think was, *Here we go again.* One of the

ABOUT THE AUTHOR

Thank you for reading this book. Every story I write has a piece of my heart attached. Here's a little bit about me... I'm a happily married mom of one snarky teenage boy and three grown "kids of my heart." As a reader and big romance fan myself, I love sharing the stories of the different people who live in my imagination. My stories are filled with humor, a few tears, and the underlying message to never give up hope, even in the darkest of times, because life can change on a dime when you least expect it. This theme comes from a lifetime of lessons learned on my own hard journey through the pains of poverty, the loss of more loved ones than I'd care to count, and the struggles of living through chronic illnesses. Life can be hard, but it can also be good! Through it all, I've found that love, laughter, and family can make all the difference, and that's what I try to bring to every tale I tell.

Would you like to receive my newsletter?
bit.ly/SusiHawkeNewsletter

The Hawke's Nest is my Facebook reader group!
www.facebook.com/groups/TheHawkesNest

www.susihawke.com

facebook.com/SusiHawkeAuthor
twitter.com/SusiHawkeAuthor
instagram.com/susi.hawke
bookbub.com/authors/susi-hawke

ALSO BY SUSI HAWKE

Shifter Series

Northern Lodge Pack Series

Northern Pines Den Series

The Blood Legacy Chronicles

Legacy Warriors

Choose Your Fate

Assassin's Claws

Desert Homesteaders

West Coast Wolves

Co-Written Shifter Series

Waking the Dragons (with Piper Scott)

Team A.L.P.H.A. (with Crista Crown)

Alphabits (with Crista Crown)

The Family Novak (with Crista Crown)

Non-Shifter Contemporary Mpreg Series

The Hollydale Omegas

MacIntosh Meadows

The Lone Star Brothers

Co-Written Omegaverse Series

Rent-a-Dom (with Piper Scott)

Three Hearts (with Harper B. Cole)

Contemporary MM Romance Series written as Susan Hawke

LOVESTRONG

Davey's Rules

Realize (Men of Hidden Creek Season 4 Book 2)

Abandoning Ship

Dancing with Daddy

News Boy

Check out my audio books!

Susi Hawke on Audible

Susan Hawke on Audible

Printed in Great Britain
by Amazon